IN SEARCH OF THE LOST TASTE
IN SEARCH OF THE LOST TASTE
IN SEARCH OF THE LOST TASTE
IN SEARCH OF THE LOST TASTE
IN SEARCH OF THE LOST TASTE
in search of the lost taste
IN SEARCH OF THE LOST TASTE
IN SEARCH OF THE LOST TASTE
IN SEARCH OF THE LOST TASTE
IN SEARCH OF THE LOST TASTE
IN SEARCH OF THE LOST TASTE

Joshua Ploeg

published by Microcosm Publishing
222 S. Rogers St. Bloomington, IN 47404
www.microcosmpublishing.com

distributed by AK Press
674-A 23rd Street
Oakland, CA 94612
(510)208-1700
sales@akpress.org

ISBN # 978-1-934620-01-4

Catalog #76065

all text by Joshua Ploeg | joshuaploeg.blogspot.com
interior illustrations by Nate Beaty | natebeaty.com
cover illustration by Aaron Renier | aaronrenier.com
art direction & graphic design by Ian Lynam | ianlynam.com

Available wholesale at standard discount through
Microcosm, AK Press, Baker & Taylor, and Ingram

A few dedications to food friends who have passed...

To my dad Henry Ploeg, an inspiration and patron of my arts. We miss him.

Joan Reeske and Eileen Humphreys, two great ladies who enjoyed many a culinary experiment from my kitchen and always provided encouragement.

John Spalding, a good friend and great chef who has always taught me to aspire higher.

Helen Hill, one of the kindest people I have ever met who also happened to throw the best Easter party I ever went to (including a bunny-shaped cake!).

My Grandma Joey Parker whose hillbilly cooking and humor showed that even the simplest things can be surprisingly complex and astute.

Grandpa Parker for putting wine in the sauce, Uncle Terry and Uncle Craig who would have enjoyed to see this all happen, and Grandpa Ploeg as well, for the "much Dutch".

And now on we go, for the living, may we all LIVE ON!
(Especially Linda, my mom- you rock, Mom!)

IN SEARCH OF THE LOST TASTE
IN SEARCH OF THE LOST TASTE
IN SEARCH OF THE LOST TASTE
IN SEARCH OF THE LOST TASTE
IN SEARCH OF THE LOST TASTE
in search of the lost taste
IN SEARCH OF THE LOST TASTE
IN SEARCH OF THE LOST TASTE
IN SEARCH OF THE LOST TASTE
IN SEARCH OF THE LOST TASTE
IN SEARCH OF THE LOST TASTE

Joshua Ploeg

TABLE *of* CONTENTS

Before we begin, you'll be putting this to use throughout the book:

Pie Crust

The basic crust for every crust in the book. You are crusty.

1 tablespoon sugar (leave it out for savory dishes)
1¼ cup presifted flour
a couple of pinches of salt
½ cup margarine
several tablespoon cold water

Mix together 1¼ cup flour with salt and tablespoon sugar. Cut in the ½ cup margarine until the mixture resembles coarse crumbs. Add water by the tablespoon (about 3 or 4), mixing in to make a good pie crust dough, and form into a ball. Chill for a bit if you wish before rolling it out. Make a double batch to be on the safe side. It's always good to have a bit laying around.

How does an adventure begin? The same as any day, albeit we adventurers may describe things well or even better than most. Let me explain the everyday in my terms.

In the culinary desert of the Central Valley (food uninspired, bland, sloppy, bad, sharp, dry, obtrusive), I had cast aside dull aspersions and sideways looks and immersed myself fully in a sensory world of food, fragrance and fun. I had turned my home into a café– not the dull wireless coffeeshop we know these days, but the classical style-center of foment and discussion, of philosophy, debate and ideas. In this sad desert, my apartment became a gastronomical oasis. Each day I prepared delicious new experiments and they came in droves to seek relief– Gnostics and Dissidents, Anarchists and Entrepreneurs, Artists, Designers, Cooks, Sculptors, Writers, Musicians, Poets, Seamsters, Weavers and Laborers, Doctors and Scientists, Creators and Destroyers.

All seeking something, perhaps finding it. They learning from me and from each other, and I from them. I felt myself fulfilled but still restless, still longing. Formless at first, a wraithlike figure began to take shape and movement during these daily and nightly soirées.

Even phantoms come to be entertained here, I thought at first. I fancied that I had it all, but the world had different fancies.

A strange shadow moved across the wall from time to time, with growing frequency, my guests oblivious. It performed a recipe, preparing it each day in the corners of my vision, the edge of my mind. It called to me. My compatriots could not see or hear this but it roared with overwhelming volume to me, ringing in my ears. What does this mean? It even began to trouble my sleep and dreams, which I value almost above food. The disturbance began to affect my cuisine itself! Unheard of!

To find the answer to the question, "what is the meaning of this commotion?", there was only one place to seek.

I left my clients with these usual items to tide them over and set out to the hut of Ms. Fortuna...

MR. SALAD WITH MUSHROOM DRESSING

1 bunch arugula, chopped
3 cups baby spinach (or some sensible amount; how do you measure that stuff?)
1 lb. cherry tomatoes, halved
1 cup chopped artichoke hearts
½ cup halved olives
1 thinly sliced red bell pepper (or any color really)
1 cup chopped cooked veggie "bacon"
½ cup of chopped fresh herbs that you wouldn't mind having in a salad– such as basil, sorrel, tarragon, etc.
1 or 2 tablespoon capers
A little minced red onion, if you like
Salt and pepper to taste
A little extra olive oil and balsamic vinegar to drizzle in addition to the dressing if necessary
Use chopped toasted slices of an herb and olive baguette as your croutons

Toss this together or arrange attractively.

Dressing: sauté ½ cup shiitake mushrooms in 2 tablespoon sesame oil with a little soy sauce and oregano until cooked. Cool and then purée with ¼ cup sun-dried tomatoes, a little salt and pepper, 2 tablespoon olive oil, 1 crushed garlic clove, 2 or 3 tablespoon lemon juice and a few tablespoon of basil leaves and use this as your dressing.

ROOT NOODLE LASAGNA WITH THREE SAUCES

White Sauce
1 lb. tofu
1 cup soy milk
¼ cup flour
5 garlic cloves, crushed
1 white onion, chopped
Handful of oregano and Italian parsley
1 teaspoon white pepper
Juice of 2 lemons
¼ cup nutritional yeast
⅓ cup olive oil
Salt to taste

Purée until smooth and set aside.

Green Sauce
2 bunches kale, chopped
1 cup red onion, chopped
2 green bell peppers, chopped
1 cup mixed herbs (marjoram, sage, rosemary and other favorites), minced
1 cup fennel or broccoli, chopped
½ cup vegetable broth
A bit of olive oil
Salt, pepper, coriander, lemon juice and paprika to taste
¼ cup flour

Add olive oil to a large skillet, add vegetables and seasonings, cook until onions begin to soften. Put in vegetable broth and cover, lower heat and cook down for 20 minutes or until kale is done, adding more liquid if necessary. Mix in flour, set aside.

Red Sauce
8 oz. tomato paste
16 oz. roasted red bell peppers
3 tablespoon flour
1 cup vegetable broth
4 garlic cloves, crushed
1 carrot, chopped
¼ cup oregano, chopped
2 tablespoon fresh rosemary
1 teaspoon paprika
¼ cup olive oil
2 bell peppers, chopped
½ cup red wine
Salt, pepper and tamari to taste

Purée all but bell peppers and wine. Cook in saucepan, adding wine and chopped pepper. Cook and stir for about 15 minutes, adjust seasonings. Set aside.

The Noodles
1 large daikon radish
2 or 3 good-sized sweet potatoes
4 potatoes, any color

Peel (if you want to) and slice all very thinly with a mandoline or your own skilled hands lengthwise (well, of reasonable length). You want them to be lasagna noodle-size. Sprinkle with salt.

Now Let's Compose This
Preheat oven to 375°. Coat a deep 9" by 13" casserole with olive oil and coat the bottom with some red sauce. Layer sweet potatoes, sprinkle with a little salt and olive oil and then lay all of the green sauce on top.

Potato layer follows, again salt and oil lightly, coat with the rest of the red sauce. On top goes the daikon, coat this with the white sauce and bake for an hour.

Top with extra white sauce, some pressed garlic and a sprinkle of nutritional yeast or your favorite vegan cheese grated. Easier than it seemed like it would be, didn't it? Want more crunch? Use jicama, it never stops being crunchy! If you don't like daikon use maybe taro root, other potatoes or yam instead, I think it adds some pep!

There will probably be too much sauce, just use it for something else!

SUGARED PLUM TARTS

Pie crust, made into 12 little balls, rolled
out into rounds, place in lightly-greased
muffin tins or ramekins. Prick them with a
fork and sprinkle with sugar.

2 cups chopped plums
1 cup sugar
½ teaspoon ground cloves
½ teaspoon ground allspice
1 teaspoon grated nutmeg
1 tablespoon vanilla
Sprinkle of sweet wine
Sprinkle of lemon juice
½ cup flour
Sprinkle of plum brandy
A few dabs of margarine

Mix together all of these ingredients and
place in your little pie shells. Bake at 425°
for 15 minutes then lower to 375° and
bake for another 10. Decorate with little
fanned plum slices with a bit of sugar and
lime juice on them.

Walnut-Pecan and Chocolate Tarts with Espresso "Cream" and Candied Sage

Make 12 little pie crusts and place in lightly-greased ramekins or muffin tins. Bake at 425° for 10 minutes.

Meanwhile...

1 cup chopped pecans
1 cup chopped walnuts
1 cup chopped chocolate
1 cup sugar
½ cup vanilla soy milk
A few tablespoon flour
Salt
Nutmeg and cinnamon if you like
¼ cup margarine
2 teaspoon vanilla
½ teaspoon baking powder

Melt margarine and chocolate in soy milk. Stir in flour, add everything else and place in pie crusts. Bake at 375° for 15 minutes more. Cool and serve with sage leaves and cream.

¼ cup espresso
¼ cup lemon juice
½ cup sugar
1 cup tofu "cream cheese"
A little vanilla

Purée/whip until smooth, add more of the cream cheese and some powdered sugar to firm it up slightly if necessary. Chill for some time before serving. It is okay for it to be more of a sauce.

Sage leaves (12–24)
1 tablespoon oil
1 cup sugar
A few tablespoon water

Heat oil, sugar and water until sugar melts and starts to bubble. Lay sage leaves in this for a minute or two, then take them out and dredge through dry sugar. Cool, then dredge again– place on top of tarts attractively.

SWEET CARROT PIE WITH CHOCOLATE SAUCE

You need the pie crust again. This time add ½ cup grated coconut and ¼ cup ground pecans and take out ½ cup of the flour at first.

2 cups grated carrots
1 cup coconut milk
½ cup flour
½ teaspoon baking powder
¾ cup sugar
Salt
¼ cup margarine
Cinnamon
Nutmeg
½ cup orange juice
2 teaspoon vanilla
½ cup medium tofu or tofu cream cheese
(add a little lemon juice)

Mix all of this together and pour into a 9" pie shell. Bake at 425° for 15 minutes then lower to 375° for another 15 or so. Allow to cool so the pie will set.

Add a little bourbon to it if you like.

1 cup chocolate
½ cup chocolate soy milk

Melt the chocolate in the choco-soy milk, stirring. Then let it cool until thickened but still saucy and serve with the pie. Add a little bourbon to it if you feel like it.

Zucchini Puffs with Tomato Butter and Caper-Herb Dressing

3 chopped zucchini
1 chopped small onion
2 minced garlic cloves
1 cup flour (or enough to make a batter
that sticks together)
1 teaspoon baking powder
¼ cup beer
1 teaspoon grated lemon peel
2 tablespoon lemon juice
½ cup chopped flat leaf parsley
¼ cup chopped oregano
Salt and pepper
1 teaspoon paprika
1 teaspoon turmeric
½ teaspoon ground cumin
Oil for frying

Mix all but the frying oil (use a tablespoon of oil in the batter), add a little water or a bit of flour if needed to make the desired consistency– a little wet for a drop batter or a little firm for shaping. Fry in hot oil, turning once, until golden brown and puffy. Drain on absorbent paper. Serve soon thereafter.

2 tablespoon margarine
¼ cup tomato paste
2 teaspoon grated onion
1 teaspoon white balsamic vinegar
salt and pepper
1 tablespoon minced parsley

Whip this up and chill. Serve on the side.

⅓ cup capers
½ cup chopped mixed herbs
2 tablespoon minced onion
1 tablespoon balsamic vinegar
2 tablespoon olive oil
Salt
A tablespoon or two of minced bell pepper and a little ginger are also nice additions
Spices: cumin and coriander are both good here

Stir all of that together and adjust seasonings. Serve with the fritters.

CHOPPED GREENS IN RED PEPPER SOUP WITH TOASTED NUTS AND FRIED ONIONS

Chopped greens: 3 heads worth of chard and collards (chop them up fairly small)
4 to 6 roasted red bell peppers
2 diced carrots
2 sliced onions and 1 diced onion
3 minced garlic cloves
1 cup chopped herbs
8 cups veggie broth
1½ teaspoon cumin
Bay leaf
1 tablespoon roasted sweet paprika
Salt and pepper
Lemon juice
Bell peppers and chili peppers (however many and whatever sort you wish)
1 cup toasted chopped mixed nuts
A few tablespoon olive oil for frying

Purée the roasted peppers with some of the broth and the spices in batches and begin to heat this with the rest of the broth, chopped onion, garlic, 1 carrot, most of the herbs, some salt and pepper, and bay leaf. Bring to a boil, then add the chopped greens and simmer for 20 minutes. Add the other carrot and the chopped peppers and cook for 10 minutes more. While that is happening, cook the sliced onions with a little salt and pepper in the olive oil until the onions start to brown. Set aside. When the soup is done, squeeze some lemon juice on there and top each individual serving with some of the leftover herbs, nuts and fried onions.

SPICY STRAWBERRY APPLESAUCE IN PASTRY CUPS WITH SWEET AND SALTY CANDIED HAZELNUTS

Phyllo dough
1 cup chopped strawberries
1½ cup chopped apples
1 cup water or apple juice mixed with a few tablespoon flour
A few tablespoon margarine
Salt and pepper
2 minced red chilies
1 small minced onion
¼ cup minced parsley
½ teaspoon coriander
½ teaspoon chili powder
½ teaspoon ground cumin
2 tablespoon minced marjoram
1 cup sugar
Lemon juice
1 cup chopped hazelnuts
A few tablespoon oil

Mix ingredients from apples through marjoram and squeeze in a little lemon juice and $\frac{1}{3}$ cup of the sugar. Cook at a simmer for 15 minutes, add strawberries and more liquid if necessary and whisk. Cook for another 10–15 minutes and re-season. If it seems too thick or too thin add more flour or liquid as needed and cook a bit longer.

Sauté the hazelnuts in oil and add a little salt and pepper and half a cup of sugar. Cook, stirring, for several minutes until sugar melts. Remove from heat and spread the nuts out on a non-stick surface until they cool a bit and dry out a little.

Cut phyllo dough into squares and press into greased muffin tins or ramekins. Baste the squares with a little oil or melted margarine and bake at 400° for 15 minutes or until browned (keep an eye on them). Allow to cool a bit and then fill each with strawberry applesauce and top with candied nuts and some minced herbs.

Baby Herb Pies
with Sun-dried Tomato Crust

1 cup chopped mixed herbs plus extra to decorate
1 cup vegan "cream cheese"
¼ cup olive oil or margarine
3 crushed garlic cloves
2 tablespoon white balsamic vinegar
Salt and pepper
1 teaspoon cumin seed
A few pinches nutmeg
½ cup chopped red onion
½ teaspoon
¼ cup flour
½ cup soy milk
Salt

Add to pie crust recipe:

½ cup chopped sun-dried tomatoes
1 tablespoon tomato paste
2 minced garlic cloves
1 teaspoon lemon juice
A bit more flour may be needed to make the crust rollable.

Blend the non-crust ingredients. Separate the crust dough into 12 or so little balls, roll them out into rounds and press them into muffin tins or ramekins. Prick with a fork and fill with the herb mixture. Bake at 400° for 15 minutes then lower to 375° for another 15 or so. Allow to cool/set a bit before serving. Decorate with some fresh herbs when done.

And so out I set with a knapsack on my back, valderi valdera all the way. To a dank and foggy bank, the edge of the Toadstool Swamps, a dangerous morass of tangled vines and becreatured waters. I paid the ferryman with a Saffron Crumpet and was promptly taken across the murky mush to the hut of Ms. Fortuna.

As I approached cautiously, apprehensively– even though I know her quite well– I heard her creaky voice wafting over the marsh, over the din of chattering twilight birds and the frogs and toads answering… "come, come adventurer, you seek my counsel again, and as usual you shall have it."

I waved aside the curtain, rattling hematite beads and jagged blocks of quartz suspended on twine and made myself comfortable.

"Yes, yes, sit, boy, I will provide your answer and what have you brought me?", she queried. I handed her some crumpets.

"And I have this for you."

She gave to me a pumpkin filled with steaming hot soup and I drank it greedily.

"You'll need the strength for the journey ahead, and now for your question: what of the phantom? Yes, yes, I know, I know as I know most things, let us see– what do the cards tell us today…".

She deftly spread the tarot with her craggy hand upon a silk cloth, waved over them once, twice, thrice and plucked three cards from the fan of wisdom.

"Fool, world, fortune," she spake… "Yes, you must make the journey, far it will take you, unknown is the outcome".

"The phantom makes a recipe, perhaps the greatest for you to seek– I cannot see for even the ball is obscured".

She waved dismissively at her crystal, off to the side, obviously shrouded in swirling mists and impenetrable.

"Perhaps this, perhaps something you did not expect, seek the trader in Metropolitan, maychance he has something that can provide a clue, now that the journey is joined you will have no rest until it is complete".

I gave her more culinary gifts, and she gave a few to me (recipes follow), then with another flourish of her hand, the whole hut, marsh and all its contents simply disappeared leaving only the faint hint of musty incense in my nostrils, and the last wafting notes of advice:

"It may be a dangerous journey for you, take care…"

I know, I know: I am in grave danger… And on to Metropolitan…

SOUP IN A PUMPKIN

A pumpkin (around 10 lbs.)
2 carrots, chopped
1 onion, diced
1 cup each chopped red and green bell pepper
1 tablespoon ginger, minced
½ cup parsley, chopped
1 tablespoon curry powder
1 teaspoon paprika
½ teaspoon each allspice, cinnamon,
nutmeg, cumin and coriander
½ cup chopped oregano, dill and cilantro
(any ratio you wish)
Salt and pepper (to taste)
1 to 2 cups coconut milk
4 cups broth
½ cup tamari roasted pumpkin seeds

Cut open the pumpkin like you're making
a jack o' lantern. Remove seeds and pulp.
Rub with oil and sprinkle with salt. Bake
at around 400° for 25 minutes with the
lid on. Meanwhile, simmer the other
ingredients (except pumpkin seeds and
a few teaspoons of the herbs) for a few
minutes, set aside. Remove pumpkin, fill
with the soup mixture and bake at 375° for
an hour in a round casserole (in case the
thing breaks). Use a foil cap instead of the
pumpkin top to bake this. Remove from
oven, take off the foil and sprinkle with
pumpkin seeds, herbs and a little paprika.
Serve soon, with the pumpkin top on when
you bring the little bugger to the table.

Lavender Soda

½ cup lavender flowers
1 cup sugar
A few tablespoon chopped crystallized
ginger
2 cups water
1 teaspoon vanilla
Soda
Lime

Bring to a boil sugar, water, lavender and
ginger. Lower to simmer and cook down
for 20 minutes to half an hour, or until it
begins to get a bit syrupy. Cool and strain,
add vanilla. You may add a bit of violet
or blue dye if you wish (natural ones are
available). Mix 1 to 3 lavender syrup to soda
water over ice in highball glasses. Garnish
with lime and a few lavender flowers.

Saffron Crumpet with Violet Jam

(You will need round cookie cutters or crumpet molds for this recipe to start the shape)

⅓ cup warm water
1 packet active dry yeast
2 cups flour
3 tablespoon sugar
1 teaspoon salt (less if desired)
¾ teaspoon baking soda
1¼ cup soy milk
1 tablespoon melted margarine or something
2 pinches of saffron
½ teaspoon turmeric

In a large bowl, stir the sugar into the warm water. Mix in the yeast and saffron and let it sit until it starts to bubble. Stir in the remaining ingredients and form into a dough. Cover and let it rise for 45 minutes in a warm place.

Pour batter into rounds on a greased, hot griddle (medium heat) and cook until the top begins to bubble, then turn and cook until done to your liking.

For jam:
Mix a cup of violets with a cup of sugar, a cup of water, a few cloves or anise stars, a small pinch of salt, 1 teaspoon oil and ½ teaspoon cornstarch. Simmer until it starts to thicken (20 minutes or so), then strain, cool and mix with some of your favorite jam.

ORANGE & VANILLA TART *with* MINT & PINEAPPLE GLAZE

2 cups chopped seeded oranges
½ cup orange juice
2 tablespoon lemon juice
1 teaspoon vanilla
1 vanilla bean's innards
1 cup tofu cream cheese
½ cup coconut milk or soy milk
½ cup flour
1 tablespoon cornstarch
A couple pinches salt
¼ teaspoon cloves
¼ teaspoon allspice
½ teaspoon orange blossom water
1½ to 2 cups sugar
½ cup chopped mint
¼ cup shredded pineapple
$^1/_3$ cup pineapple juice
A little lime juice if you wish
Pie pastry – it's that dang tart crust again!
Increase the amount of dough by a small amount for this.

Blend chopped oranges through orange blossom water, with 1 cup of the sugar, in batches if necessary. Re-season/add more sugar according to taste. Orange flavoring/ extract can be added for an orangier flavor. Roll out pie crust to fit a 10" lightly-greased pan and place the crust in that. Fill with the orange mixture and bake at 425° for 10 minutes and then lower heat to 375° and bake it for about a half an hour. Allow to cool and then chill until set.

For glaze just mix pineapple, pineapple juice and the rest of the sugar and simmer, stirring/whisking occasionally, for 10 minutes or until it thickens a bit– a little cornstarch may be whisked in to aid this process. Add half of the mint when it's ready and then cool the sauce, use the leftover for garnishing. Some sort of "whipped cream" would be good on top of these. You can of course make little tarts out of this, just don't bake them for as long.

Pumpkin Custard with Toasted Nuts, Frangelico "Cream" & Chocolate Sauce

3 cups cooked, mashed pumpkin
¼ cup margarine
1 cup tofu cream cheese
2 tablespoon lemon juice
2 cups sugar (more if you like)
A pinch or two of salt
$^1/_3$ cup flour
1 tablespoon cornstarch
1 tablespoon vanilla
1 cup chopped, toasted salted nuts (we like cashews, hazelnuts, almonds and pecans)
½ cup Frangelico
1 cup chocolate
Nutmeg
1½ cup vanilla or hazelnut soy milk

Blend pumpkin, margarine, half of the vegan cream cheese, 1 cup soy milk, nutmeg, a little salt, half of the vanilla, flour, cornstarch, 1½ cup sugar, half of the Frangelico, and if you want a little cinnamon, go for it. Bake in a lightly-greased casserole at 375° for 40–50 minutes. Cool, chill and allow to set.

Blend/whip the rest of the Frangelico, sugar, vegan cream cheese, lemon juice and chill that or even freeze it briefly (still needs to be soft though).

Melt chocolate in ½ cup soy milk with the rest of the vanilla and a little nutmeg. Cool and serve with the rest– add more liquid if it firms up too much. Put some nuts on top of each serving.

Chocolate Cake Parfait with Cocoa "Cream", Berries, Sweet Wine, Chocolate Liqueur, & Shaved Chocolate

3 cups chopped store-bought chocolate cake
2 cups mixed berries
¼ to ½ cup cocoa powder (unsweetened)
1 cup sugar
1 cup tofu cream cheese
A few tablespoon marsala
¼ cup chocolate liqueur
Piece of chocolate/chocolate bar
Lemon juice
Cinnamon
A little vanilla

This one is easy. (Did you think I was going to make you bake the cake? Fuck that!) Mix together tofu cream cheese, ½ cup sugar, cocoa powder, a dash of lemon juice and a little vanilla. Chill. Mix berries with sweet wine and a little cinnamon, sugar, maybe some grated lemon peel in there. Place some cake in each dessert cup. Sprinkle a little chocolate liqueur on. Top with a spoon of cocoa cream, then some of the berries in wine, then cover with more of the cocoa cream and grate chocolate on the top. You can break small chunks of chocolate onto the top as well; that's always fun for a variation in texture.

MASALA "CHICKEN" BALLS WITH TOASTED COCONUT, SPICY PICKLE AND LEMON-TAMARIND SAUCE

2 cups chopped veggie "chicken"
1 small minced onion
2 minced garlic cloves
½ cup chopped cilantro
¼ cup chopped basil
½ cup each chopped red and green bell pepper
2 teaspoon garam masala
1 tablespoon red curry paste
Salt and pepper
Soy sauce to taste
Chili sauce to taste
2 tablespoon lemon juice
1 tablespoon tamarind paste
1 tablespoon tomato paste
2 tablespoon mustard
1¼ cup flour (more or less as needed)
1 teaspoon baking powder
Coconut milk as your liquid
Curry breadcrumbs mixed with coconut
Oil for frying

Mix together everything up to coconut milk. Add coconut milk until you can form the mixture into some "nice balls" and make sure the seasoning is right for you. Chill the stuff for a bit, then make little balls and roll them in coconut mixed with curried breadcrumbs and fry in oil, turning if necessary, until browned.

Serve with a side of julienne spicy pickles (radish, mustard and whatnot) sprinkled with some sesame oil and mixed with a little chutney. The other sauce is easy: mix tamarind sauce with soy sauce, lemon juice and chili sauce to taste. You may need to add something sweet. (How about ginger syrup if the tamarind sauce is particularly sour?!)

FRIED STUFFED BLACK BEAN-TEMPEH PATTIES ON SEASONED GREENS WITH FRIED MUSHROOMS

Pastry (use the basic pie crust but add 1 tablespoon finely-ground sesame seeds, ½ teaspoon garlic powder, 1 teaspoon baking powder, and 2 tablespoon extra margarine. A bit more liquid may be required for rolling consistency.)
1 cup seasoned tempeh, ground and sautéed
½ cup cooked black beans
½ cup chopped green onions
A few tablespoon soy sauce
Black vinegar to taste
Sesame and peanut oil
2 cups mushrooms, chopped (mix a few kinds together)
Soy sauce
3 tablespoon sesame seeds
3 or 4 minced garlic cloves
1 head of greens, chopped
1 onion, thinly sliced
2 carrots, thinly sliced
Hot chilies (to taste), minced
Red and green bell peppers
½ teaspoon black mustard seeds
A little sweet rice vinegar
Black bean-garlic sauce
Salt and pepper
Scallions
Chili sauce
Chinese mustard

Mix together ingredients tempeh thru black vinegar. Adjust seasoning to taste, set aside (sometimes I add chopped water chestnuts and walnuts or pecans to this). Roll out dough, cut into some sort of leaf or petal pattern using your various wiles. Stuff these with tempeh mixture and fold/ seal into lovely shapes. Chill while you do the rest.

Sauté greens with onion, carrot, chilies (to taste), mustard seed, a dash of rice vinegar and bell peppers with a little salt and pepper until wilted and warm. Keep them warm!

Now you need to fry the mushrooms in enough oil to coat them, adding the minced garlic and a little soy sauce, and the sesame seeds. Fry until the seeds are for the most part browned.

Fry your stuffed petals next in some oil (it doesn't have to be a lot), turning, until browned on both sides. To compose, lay greens on a plate, followed by a few of the "petals" and some of the fried mushrooms. Decorate the whole affair with scallions, peppers and carrots. Mix black-bean sauce with either black vinegar or rice vinegar and the chili sauce with mustard for some dipping sauces to have on the side.

Grapefruit, Orange and Fennel Salad with Veggie "Crab" in Pastry Cups

1 or 2 grapefruit
1 or 2 oranges
1 fennel bulb
A few teaspoon white wine vinegar
1 tablespoon chili sauce
1 tablespoon freshly-grated horseradish
A few tablespoon French or Russian dressing (if you want)
A few tablespoon olive oil
A squeeze of lime juice
Salt and pepper
A few tablespoon each minced dill, cilantro and marjoram
A few tablespoon seaweed flake
Some beet juice and beet powder
1 cup light colored veggie "meat" (more if you like)
Pastry (I like phyllo, make it a thickness of four sheets to handle this filling)

Cut the pastry into squares and bake in greased muffin tins or ramekins at 425° for 15 minutes. Allow to cool and then stuff with the salad, which can be mixed or an "arrangement".

Take the fake meat, soak in some beet juice, salt and seaweed flakes for a while, drain and cook in a little oil until it starts to brown. Remove and cool, then shred it and sprinkle with more seaweed flake and a little beet powder and old bay or crab boil spice and chill. Section the grapefruit and oranges and cut them in half, slice the fennel very thinly. Dress these with the herbs, olive oil, lime juice, vinegar, salt and pepper. You can arrange all of this in the cups and then mix chili sauce, horseradish and French or Russian dressing together and put on the side decoratively, or toss it all together.

The hustle of the city wreaked havoc on my preoccupied mind. It seemed as though I was nearly run over (by traffic as well as by pedestrians!) at every corner. The sensory overload of flashing lights, loud, almost-random blaring sound, and of course the vast labyrinth of all too vivid food smells – hot dogs, pho, crepes, cupcakes, French fries, vindaloo sauce, croissants (a little late for that i'n it?), mustard and BBQ. So much… Too much… My head was ready to explode… And I was ravenous to boot.

To top it all off, I couldn't shake the feeling that I was being followed… Perhaps the crone was right– it could be something more than I expected. Just as I was about to pass out from yet another whiff of stale buns and an explosion of condiments in the air, I managed to stagger into the curio shop of Mr. Wyse.

The door flew open, the salty wind roared, knocking half the nearest knicknacks off their shelves, and the little bells rang… *dingdong dingdong*… and thus I was announced.

Mr. Wyse, his usual scattered self, came falling out of the middle of several great towers of mildewed boxes and tripped into me, adjusting his broken spectacles. I barely had my own druthers but managed to hold him up precariously by the arms, as he leaned into me, barely suspended in this awkward position.

"Yes of course my boy, well met, again, you seem healthy, yes, of course what can I do for you?"

"Mmm… Ms. Fortuna you say? Phantom? Great recipe? Oh my oh my, w-w-well… as you can see I was just unpacking a new ship-ship-shipment and I think I have just, just, just the thing for you!".

He fell backwards, headlong into the stacks which then became a pile– waving his arms, boxes flying everywhere, exclamations and grunting. Just as I reached out to help the poor fellow up, out from the cardboard jungle shot his arm, extended with a small clay idol in his hand. "H-h-here, t-t-take it, a small god of kitchen arts– from an an ancient land, this must be what you are here for, I say! I knew it would be im-im-important when I first laid eyes on it. On it."

I took it, paid the poor Mr. Wyse a pittance pie, thanked him, gave him some ice cream, then returned to the bustling streets.

What the hell is this thing? I eyed the small idol, looking for any clue as to where its importance lay. Nothing. God of the kitchen? I say!

I couldn't wrap my mind about this puzzle on an empty stomach so I went to the best restaurant I could find and ate these things that follow.

Afterwards I was so happy and high I couldn't contain myself, I jumped for joy. Without thinking I picked up the idol and smashed it on the sidewalk. Oh dear, oh no- what have I done?!… but wait… hold on a minute… what's this?… ho ho what is this…? Amongst the miniature rubble I had created– here's a little scroll. Well, already you fool, unroll it– it's a map! Of course, a map and well, where does it take me? Let's see, I don't read much in the way of glyphs but it looks like it says… "The Valley of Kings, Wings n Things"– the tombs of the Culinary Pharoahs– oh no!

Spicy Chilled Tomatoes in Sake Vinaigrette

3 cups tomatoes, sliced
2 to 4 minced hot green and red chilies
2 tablespoon seasoned rice vinegar
¼ cup dry sake
1 tablespoon grated ginger
Salt and pepper
2 tablespoon sesame oil
1 tablespoon mustard oil (or whatever)
2 or 3 lime leaves
1 teaspoon crushed green peppercorns
herbs: garlic chives or scallions, basil,
watercress, a little flaked seaweed might
be nice.

I also go for a little ground toasted sesame
seed with a bit of salt in it

Additions: grated daikon or burdock root,
popped mustard seeds (do that in a little
oil with some salt)

Use an interesting variety of tomatoes. Mix all
together and chill. Serve using a slotted spoon,
mix again and re-season before serving.

LEMONGRASS-BASIL "ICE CREAM"

2 cups coconut milk
1 cup sugar
1 tablespoon lemongrass (more to taste)
1 cup chopped basil
1 small minced Thai chili
innards of 1 vanilla bean
½ cup mango juice
½ cup lime juice
2 tablespoon gin
½ cup soy creamer
A pinch or two of salt

Melt sugar in soy creamer over low-med heat with lemongrass, stirring occasionally. Cool and then blend in batches with the rest of the ingredients. Freeze until firm, making sure to give it a good stir every half hour or so– so that it won't ice up too terribly. It takes a while to freeze properly, so give yourself some time on this one and make sure your freezer works properly.

CHERRY WONTONS WITH PLUM-BRANDY SAUCE AND YAM-MANGO "ICE CREAM"

1 cup pitted, drained cherries
1 tablespoon flour
A little margarine
½ cup sugar
A pinch salt
½ teaspoon vanilla
2 teaspoon minced ginger
Wonton/eggroll wrappers
Oil for frying

Mix cherries thru ginger and make wontons or "eggrolls" with the wrappers, use about a tablespoon of filling each (only if the wrappers are large). Make sure they are tightly sealed. I would fry in fairly shallow oil and just turn them since no matter what you do some sort of cherry juice leaks out. Cook and turn until they are nicely browned, drain on absorbent paper and sprinkle with cinnamon sugar.

For sauce, purée:
1 cup chopped plums, ½ teaspoon ground cloves, 1 teaspoon allspice, ½ cup brandy, 2 teaspoon cornstarch, ½ cup sugar, ½ cherry juice, ½ teaspoon vanilla.
Heat, stirring until somewhat thickened.

Yam-Mango Ice Cream

2 cups cooked yams, chopped (still warm)
1 ½ cup sugar (use more or less to taste)
2 cups coconut milk
1 cup orange-mango juice
1 cup mango, chopped
2 teaspoon lemon juice
1 teaspoon cinnamon, ground
2 teaspoon ginger, minced
2 tablespoon bourbon or rum (a flavoring will suffice)

Blend all in batches and pour into container.

Freeze, stirring occasionally.

FRUIT TARTS *with* SESAME CRUST AND GINGER GLAZE

3 peeled, sliced kiwis
2 chopped mangos
1 cup sliced strawberries
½ cup blueberries
½ cup sugar
1 teaspoon toasted, lightly-salted sesame seeds
2 tablespoon grated ginger
¼ cup fruit juice
2 tablespoon flour (if you're going to cook it)
Optional: a little of the ol' vegan cream cheese
Pie crust except replace ¼ cup of the flour with ¼ cup sesame seeds, add a teaspoon of powdered ginger and dust the board with rice flour. Roll out fairly thin.

Cut the pie crust into 12 squares and press into lightly-greased muffin tins. Prick with a fork. Mix the other stuff together and scoop into the crusts. Bake at 425° for 10 minutes then lower the temperature to 375° for another 10 to 15 minutes. Allow to cool on a wire rack, then carefully remove them. Decorate with extra fruit. If you do the cream cheese, put that under the fruit before you bake with a little sugar sprinkled on board.

The other way, bake the crusts for 15 minutes or until done, then put the mixed fruit in raw. More refreshing that way, just be sure it's not too juicy!

PEANUT BREADED AND FRIED MARINATED TEMPEH WITH GARLIC-LIME SAUCE

2 lbs. tempeh
1½ cup ground peanuts
½ cup rice flour
A little chili powder
A few tablespoon flour
Sesame or peanut oil
Lime juice
Soy sauce
Rice vinegar
Chili sauce
Garlic
Salt and pepper
Oil for frying
Option: sprinkle the tempeh with a little garam masala or a Thai spice mix before coating in peanut flour

Cut tempeh into triangles and marinate for a while in soy sauce, lime juice, rice vinegar, chili sauce, minced garlic, pepper and onion and some oil– turn every now and then and add more of the ingredients as the tempeh soaks it up. Grind peanuts into crumbs/flour consistency with a little salt and pepper and chili powder, mix in rice flour and flour. Take the tempeh triangles and coat them in the peanut flour mixture and fry them in oil, turning as needed, until browned.

Serve with this delicious lime sauce:

¼ cup minced cilantro
¼ cup minced basil
½ cup lime juice
1 teaspoon cornstarch
Several tablespoon peanut oil or sesame oil
¼ cup shredded lime
2 teaspoon grated lime peel
A little soy sauce
A whole bulb of minced garlic
Salt and pepper
Chili sauce to taste
Option: Add toasted coconut and a little more oil

Brown the garlic in oil with a little salt and soy sauce. Add lime juice mixed with cornstarch and stir (watch out for the splatter!), then remove from heat after a couple of minutes and add everything else.

FRIED BASIL CAKES WITH TAMARIND HOT SAUCE AND COCONUT JELLY

rice syrup, 2 tablespoon tamarind paste or tamarind sauce, 1 teaspoon soy sauce and ¼ cup water.

2 cups chopped Thai basil
1 sliced onion
3 minced garlic cloves
2 tablespoon minced ginger
Pepper and salt
2 or 3 tablespoon Chinese vinegar
2 tablespoon rice vinegar
1 or 2 tablespoon green curry paste
1 cup flour (more as needed)
1 teaspoon baking powder
1 diced carrot
1 chopped bell pepper
½ cup chopped cilantro
2 or 3 tablespoon chili sauce
1 tablespoon grated galangal
Liquid to form a wet batter (try coconut milk)
Oil for frying

Mix all that but the frying oil together, adding liquid or flour as needed to make a nice drop batter, adjust the seasonings– it should taste a little crazy. Fry ¼ cup amounts of this in modest/moderate oil, turning once, until browned on both sides. You can flatten them out a bit when cooking to make the shape correct if you need to.

Blend ½ cup shredded coconut, salt (to taste), sugar (to taste), ½ cup coconut milk, 1 teaspoon cornstarch, 1 teaspoon ginger– heat to a simmer, then chill.

Blend thoroughly 2 tablespoon chili sauce, 1 tablespoon lemon juice, 2 tablespoon

THICK RICE NOODLES *with* SPICY "BEEF", FRIED CABBAGE, SCALLION, PEPPERS, IN GARLIC SAUCE

1 pkg. dry wide rice noodles
2 tablespoon black vinegar
¼ cup soy sauce
2 sliced onions
3 minced scallions
2 cups shredded cabbage
1 lb. chopped fake "beef" strips/tempeh/tofu/seitan
2 chopped green bell peppers (or other colors)
2 or 3 minced hot chilies
3 minced garlic cloves
¼ cup each chopped cilantro and basil
¼ cup sesame oil
1 cup sliced shiitake mushrooms
A little five-spice
Chili sauce
Canola, corn or peanut oil
Additions: toasted sesame seeds, pickled mustard greens, radish pickle, preserved black beans, chopped roasted peanuts

Begin by frying up onions, fake meat, garlic, chilies, some spice and soy sauce (a couple tablespoon of it now) in a little mix of peanut and sesame oil. Cook for a few minutes, then add cabbage, bell peppers, mushrooms, and a little more seasonings. Meanwhile, boil and drain the noodles. After the mixture with the cabbage and such has cooked for a few minutes toss in the noodles, herbs, scallions, black vinegar and more soy sauce, chili sauce and sesame oil. Also add whatever additions you like to the whole business and season to taste. Basically this is just Chow Fun but we love it.

Pineapple Eggroll

1½ cup chopped or shredded, drained
pineapple
½ cup minced red bell pepper
1 or 2 minced green chilies
1 or 2 minced scallions
1 minced garlic clove
1 tablespoon minced ginger
¼ cup chopped basil
¼ cup chopped cilantro
A tablespoon or so soy sauce
A sprinkle of rice vinegar or lime juice
½ teaspoon grated lime peel (more if you
like the stuff)
1 tablespoon rice flour or regular flour
1 teaspoon toasted sesame seeds
if you like, a little chili sauce or other fun
sauce in there
2 teaspoon sesame oil
1 teaspoon or so of fun spices– five-spice, a
curry powder, or what have you
wonton/eggroll wrappers
oil for frying
Optional additions: fake meat, seasoned
tofu or cooked mushrooms, toasted or
popped mustard seeds, chopped toasted
cashews or macadamia nuts

Mix everything but the cooking oil and
wrapper together. Roll a tablespoon or two
of the filling in each wrapper, seal tightly
and fry until browned and done. Serve
with a couple of sauces, I would do peanut,
something soy sauce-y, a chili sauce, and/
or a chutney.

Bamboo, Radish, Leek Hearts and Fried Gluten In Spicy Coconut Milk Sauce

1 cup chopped fresh bamboo
½ cup chopped chili radish
2 chopped leek hearts
1 cup chopped curry gluten/fake meat
1 or 2 teaspoon of a rich red curry powder
(or a tablespoon of paste)
Soy sauce to taste
Couple tablespoon chili-garlic sauce
1 cup coconut milk
Salt and pepper
1 sliced onion
2 minced garlic cloves
¼ cup sesame oil (to fry, and drizzle)
1 tablespoon sugar or rice syrup
1 teaspoon chili powder
½ cup chopped cilantro (add basil if you like)
1 tablespoon grated galangal root
1 tablespoon minced lemongrass
1 bay leaf

This is easy, start by frying the gluten, onions, ginger, bay leaf and garlic with some soy sauce (to taste) and red curry powder. When the gluten starts to brown, add everything else (save half of the cilantro) and simmer for 10 minutes. Add more cilantro, re-season and serve as a side dish, drizzled with a little sesame oil.

Straw Mushroom and Black Sesame Rolls with Spicy Mustard Sauce and Sweet Black Vinegar-Soy Sauce

1½ cup chopped straw mushrooms
1 cup crumbled tofu
¾ cup flour (more as needed)
1 teaspoon baking powder
Salt and pepper to taste
1 or 2 tablespoon soy sauce
1 tablespoon Chinese black vinegar
1 tablespoon sesame oil
⅓ cup chopped onion
3 cloves minced garlic
¼ cup chopped basil
2 tablespoon mustard
1 tablespoon chili sauce
2 teaspoon plus some to coat black sesame seeds
Rice flour (season it)

Mix all but rice flour and extra sesame seeds together, kneading and adding flour if you must until this batter has a nice almost uniform texture. Break pieces off and roll in rice flour and sesame seeds and fry in some oil, turning, until browned on all sides. Drain on absorbent paper and serve with sauce.

These sauces are simple condiment combinations:
Mix equal parts soy sauce and Chinese black vinegar for one, add a few toasted regular sesame seeds to it.
For the other, blend a few tablespoon Dijon mustard with a little hot Chinese mustard, and a tablespoon or two of chili garlic sauce. Add a squeeze of lemon or lime juice.

Blast this foul, dusty desert! Swatting flies, all of my treats covered in sand, on the back of a stinky camel humping to and fro, I scarcely have an appetite. Where is this godforsaken tomb?

Well, I have perhaps a bit of hunger at any rate, so I'll eat this little Pistachio Roll. Now, to find a shelter to enjoy it undisturbed by all of these uninvited particles. Oh here, perhaps I'll just sit under this mantle and lean back and enjoy... Whoa!

I tumbled seemingly endlessly backwards down some bone- and cobweb-strewn shaft, thrown down until... Wham! I found myself on the stone floor of some accursed room. As I got my feet about me, scattered light filtered through the dust from down the shaft creating an almost evanescent glow. Sarcophagi, obsidian cats, daggers, gold (!) glittered all about the room. Jewels, tapestries and mysterious glyphs. Bronze and gilded pots and pans, whisks and plates– could this be?

Something stirred, I shivered. Something shuffled, I squirmed. Something grunted, then growled. Panicked, I began jumping up, trying to scramble back up the shaft. No good– some unholy, fetid hand had me by the leg and threw me back down to the ground. The menacing mummified face of the ungodly monster met mine... not

like this! I'm gonna have my last meal if it's the last thing I do! The Pistachio Roll still in my hand, I put it to my mouth for the final taste when the mummy, his hand raised to strike mercilessly and end my life, suddenly hesitated. He sniffed... and sniffed again. Then came the unmistakable sound... "ahhh".

Hungry? He nodded sadly– I offered him the roll which he proceeded to devour with relish as though he had not eaten in ten thousand years. He leaned back, took in a big breath, sighed, and then laughed sagely.

"Truly you have broken the curse at last– ah you are curious? Another great cook, jealous of my deeds, conspired to have me prematurely entombed and to never taste another bite of living food for all of eternity! But you, come here it seems by fate rather than chance, have ceased my torments so treacherously laid by my enemy– and in such fashion! Tell me what it is that you seek, for I can certainly tell that you are on a quest my friend... What's this?"

He snatched the scroll from my trembling fingers.

"Ah, indeed! A bit of a kitchen spelunker by trade I take it, seeking fame and fortune. Hmmm, well your culinary knowledge I hope exceeds your map-reading skill– you have the tomb, here, certainly, but under this stain here, when held to the light or open flame, here you see the true destination– you must cross the mountains of AnIstan."

He tossed the paper back at me dismissively.

"Oh, and I thank you for the treat. Have you any else? Or some ingredients perhaps– there are all manner of recipes ancient and wise in this tomb, sealed forever and I forever unable to make them! Perhaps now this has changed, I hope, for I am certainly hungry!" he bemoaned.

Hmmm, maybe I can help with some parting gifts of gratitude for such a high-ranking patron.

"And what do I eat then? Well, see this dratted curse for yourself…"

He gestured toward an ornate golden table inlaid with seraphs and other winged beasts…

There preserved before me was an embalmed feast. The poor old dirty Pharoah truly had not a scrap to eat!

Although beautiful, what good is this buffet when it can only be eaten with the eyes? Surely the stomach hungers as well, even in the afterlife! Well before I went on my way I set about to recreate his favorite dishes for him to enjoy, and here they are…

BUTTER BEAN-ROASTED EGGPLANT DIP

Chop an eggplant, coat in olive oil, lemon juice and sprinkle with salt and a few tablespoon water and roast at 375° in a pan in the oven for half an hour.

Remove and purée with the following:

1½ cup cooked butter beans
½ cup tofu creem cheeze
¼ cup lemon juice
¼ cup unsweetened soy milk (more if needed)
Salt and pepper to taste (lots of salt!)
2 tablespoon tahini (more to taste)
2 or 3 tablespoon olive oil
A pinch of cumin
A bit of dill and parsley, nice and fresh
¼ cup onion
4 to 8 garlic cloves, peeled and smashed

Adjust seasonings to taste, blend until smooth. This makes a good amount of it. Serve with bread or crackers for nice snack.

Cinnamon-Pepper Tea

Steep black or herbal tea (2 bags to the pot) with 2 cinnamon sticks (broken), 8 crushed black peppercorns, 2 lemon slices, 6 crushed cardamom pods, and a handful of mint for about 10 minutes. Strain into cups and serve with a little sugar, mint and a cinnamon stick.

STONE DRAGGER'S SALAD

2 cups cooked pearl barley (or bulgur!)
½ cup chopped roasted red bell peppers
½ cup chopped parsley
¼ cup chopped mint
½ cup pitted olives
2 tomatoes, cut into thin half slices
1 red onion, diced
2 diced or sliced carrots

Mix together, then add this dressing:

2 cloves garlic, minced
¼ cup tahini
2 tablespoon balsamic vinegar
¼ cup lemon juice
1 tablespoon soy sauce
2 tablespoon olive oil
2 tablespoon water or so
Salt and pepper to taste
A little sumac, and how about a dash of
Spike or other seasoning

TOFU, DATE AND PISTACHIO ROLLS WITH SWEET AND SPICY PEPPER SAUCE

Phyllo dough
½ cup chopped dates
1 lb. fried seasoned tofu, diced
½ cup roasted salted pistachios
$^1/_3$ cup minced red onion
a few tablespoon minced herbs (I like dill, oregano and parsley here)
2 tablespoon balsamic vinegar
1 tablespoon date or palm sugar
1 teaspoon flour
red chili flake to taste
1 orange bell pepper, minced
1 small orange: peeled, seeded and cut into pieces
Turmeric, coriander, cumin, fennel seed, cinnamon (to taste, start with ½ teaspoon each)
Salt and pepper, soy sauce/tamari to taste
Olive oil and/or a few tablespoon of margarine

Mix together all but phyllo dough and oil. Season to taste, add a little oil or dots of margarine. Cut phyllo dough sheets in half. Place a tablespoon of filling on each cut sheet and roll as though doing eggrolls, tightly. Bake on greased cookie sheets at 425°, baste the rolls with melted margarine or oil before baking, for 20 minutes or a bit longer until nicely browned.

Serve with this sauce:

A few hot chilies
1 cup mixed roasted peppers
2 tablespoon chili sauce
1 tablespoon olive oil
½ cup apricot or tangerine juice
A little sugar
½ teaspoon each turmeric, paprika and chili powder
1 carrot
1 or 2 tablespoon lemon juice or red wine vinegar
1 garlic clove
2 tablespoon onion
1 teaspoon flour or potato starch or cornstarch

Purée this and heat to a simmer, stirring. Cook until a little thickened, adjust seasonings to taste.

Pistachio Breaded Tofu with Tangerine Sauce

1 lb. extra firm or baked tofu, cut into triangles
¼ cup soy sauce
1 cup salted roasted pistachios, ground into a flour
½ cup flour
½ teaspoon baking powder
salt and pepper to taste
1 teaspoon chili powder
1 teaspoon turmeric
2 minced garlic cloves
A little garlic and onion powder to taste
Some minced herbs (dill, oregano, or whatever)
Oil for frying

Mix the tofu triangles with a little oil (tablespoon or so), herbs, minced garlic and soy sauce. Let sit for a little bit. Mix the rest except frying oil together and then toss with the tofu until well coated. Fry triangles in oil, turning, until browned all about. Sprinkle with some nice seasoning mix that you like (if you think it won't be too salty).

Serve with this sauce:

1 cup tangerine (peeled, seeded, chopped)
½ cup tangerine juice
A little cornstarch or flour
1 tablespoon lemon juice
⅓ cup sugar
¼ cup minced onion

2 teaspoon grated ginger
2 cloves pressed garlic
A little curry powder (1 teaspoon or so)
1 tablespoon oil
Salt to taste

Heat in a saucepan, stirring with a whisk and simmer until a bit thicker. Sometimes I add apricot jelly or tangerine preserve to this. Season to taste.

Sprinkle the whole business with chopped Italian parsley, that's always nice.

SPINACH AND ALMOND-BURGUNDY OLIVE TAPENADE PASTRIES

Phyllo dough
2 tablespoon capers
1 cup chopped pitted olives (I like burgundy olives or kalamata here)
½ cup diced white onion
4 minced garlic cloves
2 or 3 tablespoon balsamic vinegar
A few tablespoon olive oil
Salt and pepper to taste, of course
A few tablespoon each minced thyme, oregano, dill and flat parsley
A few hot and bell peppers, minced
1 cup chopped spinach leaves
Tamari roasted almonds, chopped
2 diced tomatoes
A little flour (1 or 2 tablespoon)
1 teaspoon paprika

Mix all but the phyllo dough together, save a little oil too. Discover the method of folding that will help you turn a sheet of phyllo into a triangle or square encasing about 2 tablespoon of the mixture. If a whole sheet seems cumbersome, cut in half.

Place the pastries on greased baking pans/sheets and bake at 425° (make sure to baste the pastries with a little oil, sprinkle also with some paprika) for 20 to 25 minutes or until browned (keep an eye on them). If it takes longer, your oven is not hot enough!

This is best served with leftover of the inside mixture (minus the flour) and any of those white garlic-dill sauces I have in here.

Whole Fava Beans in Spicy Tomato Sauce

Use a mix totalling 2 tablespoon of these
ground up together: cinnamon, chili
powder, cumin, coriander, paprika, cloves,
fenugreek, mustard seed, ground ginger
3 cups fava beans (use shelled fresh or
frozen ones, not dried. Canned is fine too)
1 cup diced or ground tomatoes
1 or 2 tablespoon tomato paste
a few chopped hot and bell peppers
1 diced onion
3 minced garlic cloves
A handful of chopped herbs (oregano, dill
or what have you)
Some chopped fenugreek leaves
½ cup chopped parsley
1 bay leaf
¼ cup lemon or lime juice
A few tablespoon olive oil
Broth as needed
Optional: Add some fresh chopped onion
as a topping to each serving

Begin frying the onions, bay leaf, and garlic
in oil for 2 minutes. Add the fava beans
and peppers and a little salt and pepper
and cook briefly. Add tomatoes, then spices,
tomato paste, herbs and about half a cup
of broth. Cook for 20 minutes at a simmer,
keep a partial cover on and add liquid if
it starts to dry out. Add some lemon juice
and adjust seasonings. Cook for another
5 minutes or so, then finish with some
more lemon juice and fenugreek leaves
and parsley (stir some of these in and
also sprinkle some on top of each serving).
Serve hot/warm with some pita bread.

BROAD BEAN AND POTATO PUREÉ IN GARLIC BROTH WITH MINCED HERBS

2 cups cooked broad beans, mashed
2 cups cooked potatoes, mashed
2 diced onions
4 cloves minced garlic
¼ cup chopped dill
1 tablespoon chili sauce
2 cups broth with 2 minced garlic cloves added
A few tablespoon tahini mixed with juice of half a lemon
A handful of mixed chopped herbs (parsley, oregano, a little rosemary is nice) to taste, try a pinch of saffron and half a teaspoon of the rest to start: turmeric, ginger, coriander, fenugreek, saffron, cardamom
salt and pepper to taste

Put it all in a pot and heat to a simmer, stirring ambitiously to incorporate it all into one great mess. Cook for 20 minutes, season to taste. It's probably done but you can add more seasoning and cook it further if desired. Garnish with parsley, some tomatoes if you like, lemon wedges, all that fun stuff.

You should serve it with that nice bread you learned earlier.

FRIED BREADED GARLIC "CHICKEN" WITH OLIVES IN ROASTED PEPPER CREAM SAUCE, AND APRICOT ORZO

Veggie "chicken" pieces (a lb. or two—whatever grand variety you enjoy the most and in whatever shape)

Coat it with some soy sauce and minced garlic and a little melted margarine or oil, then dredge in breadcrumbs with sage, parsley, oregano, salt and pepper and paprika in it (taste them, it should taste good already).

Fry these in a modest amount of oil until browned on both sides (yes, you will turn it, my clever turnip). Then place it in a greased baking dish with a chopped onion, a cup of pitted kalamata or green olives (or mix) and a few whole garlic cloves. Top with 3 or 4 lemon slices and put in the oven at 325° until you have finished the rest of your business, which is...

Purée this, my dear, and then heat it in a saucepan:
1 teaspoon paprika, turmeric, chili powder, cumin and coriander
1 cup hot and red bell peppers (roasted)
¼ cup lemon juice
1 cup tofu cream cheese
½ cup broth
Salt and pepper to taste
¼ cup minced oregano, parsley and dill
2 garlic cloves

Cook some orzo according to the instructions but add a handful of chopped apricots and some chopped onion to it. When it is done, drain it and toss with margarine (or something healthier) and a bit of minced Italian parsley.

Serve with sauce and that nice veggie chicken from the oven that you have almost forgotten about!

PLUM *and* PISTACHIO CRISP *with* OUZO-LEMON "ICE CREAM" *and* ROSE SYRUP

4 cups chopped plums
$1/3$ cup flour
½ cup sugar (more as needed)
A pinch of salt
1 teaspoon cinnamon, ½ teaspoon cloves
1½ teaspoon vanilla extract
¼ cup margarine, cut up
A dash rose water
1 cup roasted pistachios
½ cup slivered almonds
¼ cup pomegranate juice
2 tablespoon lemon juice

Mix this casually and put it in a lightly-greased baking pan or casserole (not too deep) with plums.

Top with:
½ cup flour
1 cup ground modestly-salted pistachios (no shells!)
½ cup sugar
½ cup (or a bit less) margarine or similar substance
½ teaspoon baking powder
1 teaspoon cinnamon
A little nutmeg.

Mix together.

Bake at 375° for 40 minutes or so until the top is browned.

For your Ice Creem, blend: ¼ cup ouzo, 1 teaspoon grated lemon peel, ¼ cup sugar, a can of frozen lemonade, ½ cup soy creamer (vanilla works), ½ cup coconut milk and a pinch or two of salt until smooth, and freeze, stirring it up occasionally to make sure it doesn't get too hard.

For syrup, this is easy– Mix a half cup of lemon sugar syrup (like soda flavoring) with a teaspoon of rose water, a few minced rose petals, and a pinch of cardamom (maybe a little salt) and warm, serve over it all.

This is almost worse than the desert– loping jagged mountains, everybody covers their face– I can't even tell who's hot I just have to guess. Egad! Again with the dust and dirt as well and on donkey back to boot, how undignified. Am I still being followed? I could swear someone is watching me, I could…What is that smell? Yak milk? Are you serious? Oh, well hey that's not all bad after all– shut my mouth! At least the food is good, and the people are friendly. Hmmm… not sure where I'm going but this friendly family has taken me in for the night in this small, quaint village. "Come traveler, rest. You must be near your destination, from this map. It is grand that we can be part of this culinary quest. You are like, how do you say 'Lancelot'. Okay! Lance, I am a bit cook myself, shall we share a few dishes? Welcome to my kitchen!" Glorious! Such great large pots and pans, and what a fine hearth with the bread baking already! The smells, fresh herbs, spices, oh goodie I can't wait.

Nice music. Hey, let's make a fantastic feast together; you show me something of yours and I'll show you mine! Oh, what fun, recipes from this untamed place follow of course.

Oh yes, indeed I'm having such a great time up here and feel so welcome, the journey is at an end– what could possibly interfere with perfection? Oh, is that tea?

Well, who is that strange cloaked gentleman gesturing to me at that door over there that I didn't notice before. Maybe I should follow him– what a top idea!…

"Psst! This way. I must tell you the location. Yes, yes, I know it. What you seek, where to find it– No no, not in this insignificant hamlet. This way, yes, follow follow, just a bit further and NOW!"

Oompfh! Burlap goes over the head… I've been bagged… punched in the stomach then batted on the head…. I've been tagged!

Faint cries off in the distance of "Lance, Lance, where you are?"

And the lights go out…

Quick Vegetable Pot

2 cups whole button mushrooms
2 zucchini, cut into thick slices
1 cup chard, cut into ribbons
1 diced or sliced onion
4 cloves of minced garlic
Soy sauce, salt and pepper to taste
1 teaspoon each cumin, sesame seeds,
coriander and sumac
A few tablespoon of olive or sesame oil
½ cup chopped parsley
2 chopped tomatoes (or cut into wedges)
2 fresh lemons

Cook mushrooms, zucchini, chard, onions,
garlic and spices in oil for a couple of
minutes, add soy sauce, salt and pepper
and cover. Cook for 5 minutes. Add the
parsley and tomato, juice of lemon (as
much as you like). Toss and remove from
heat. Serve immediately.

GREEN BREAD

2 cups flour
4 sliced garlic cloves
½ teaspoon to 1 teaspoon salt
2 packets active dry yeast
½ teaspoon baking powder
2 tablespoon lemon juice
2 tablespoon nutritional yeast
¼ cup chopped parsley
¼ cup chopped cilantro
¼ cup chopped green onions
2 tablespoon olive oil
½ cup warm water
Activate the yeast in warm water. Add
everything else and form into a dough,
using more flour if necessary. Allow to rise,
covered, for 1 hour. Separate into small
balls and roll out thinly into 8" rounds. Cook
on a griddle, lightly-greased with olive oil,
turning once, until browned on both sides.
Sprinkle with sea salt and garlic powder.

Cashew-Sesame Shake

1 cup roasted cashews
¼ cup sesame seeds
¼ cup sugar or sugar syrup (more to taste)
2 cups soy milk, almond milk, thin coconut
or a mix (I go for the coconut)
½ teaspoon cardamom
Pinch of salt
Innards of a vanilla bean or 1 teaspoon vanilla
Also good: a little rose water or saffron

Liquefy and chill. Serve over ice/strain
if you like. You can also make it more
yogurty tasting with an extra pinch of salt
and use ¼ cup lemon juice to replace some
of the milk substance.

LENTILS, SORREL, RADISHES AND GREENS IN HERB AND LEMON DRESSING

2 cups cooked mixed lentils (cook them in a
tasty vegetable or mushroom broth and drain)
1 cup chopped sorrel
¼ cup minced red onion
Salt and pepper to taste
1 cup sliced radishes
2 diced carrots
2 peppers (try 1 red, 1 orange), chopped
1 cup chopped flat-leafed parsley (it's
always flat-leafed Italian parsley with me!)
1 head spinach, chopped
1 tablespoon each minced thyme and oregano
¼ cup minced dill
1 teaspoon fennel seed
2 teaspoon Middle-Eastern spice mix
(kebab mix, i like it!)
¼ cup red wine vinegar
A few tablespoon olive oil
¼ cup lemon juice
1 teaspoon toasted, ground sesame seeds
with a little salt
1 tablespoon finely grated ginger
1 lemon, thinly sliced

Mix together, season to taste and serve. I
would sprinkle it with sumac. Top with the
lemon slices, they help to flavor the dish. It
is also good with roasted or fried eggplant or
zucchini on it and some fresh tomato slices.

Semolina and Carrot Soup with Ginger-Lemon Broth and Pistachios

7 cups broth
1 cup chopped herbs (dill, parsley, oregano, etc. together)
2½ lbs. chopped or sliced carrots
6 cloves sliced garlic
4 lemon slices and ⅓ cup lemon juice
2 tablespoon grated ginger
2 bay leaves
¼ cup chives
2 white onions, diced
1 cup semolina
Salt and pepper
2 teaspoon turmeric, 2 pinches saffron, 1 teaspoon cumin, 1½ teaspoon coriander and ½ teaspoon cardamom
A little olive oil
1 cup chopped roasted, salted pistachios

Simmer the broth with half of the herbs, half the ginger, half the spice, one of the onions, 2 of the garlic cloves, bay leaves and a half lb. of the carrots for 30 minutes. Strain and simmer again, with everything else (save half of the pistachios and the chives for garnish), for 20 minutes. Adjust seasoning to taste, garnish with chives and pistachios.

Djinn's Delicious Dates

20 dates
½ cup vegan "cream cheese"
2 tablespoon chopped roasted salted cashews
2 tablespoon apricot preserve
1 tablespoon marmelade
Salt
1 or 2 teaspoon lemon juice
chopped cilantro

Mix together all but the dates and cilantro. Split the dates open on one side and remove the pits. Stuff with the mixture and place on a platter. Sprinkle with cilantro and chill.

DEEP-FRIED BREADED APRICOT "BEEF'" BALLS WITH SPICY SWEET RELISH AND MUSTARD

2 cups veggie "ground beef"
½ cup chopped dried apricots
¼ cup mustard
1 tablespoon curry powder
½ cup minced onions
¼ cup chopped cilantro
¼ cup chopped herbs (I like dill and marjoram, and also parsley)
2 tablespoon tomato paste
1 cup or so flour
Tablespoon each olive and sesame oil
1½ teaspoon baking powder
Couple tablespoon sugar
Salt and pepper
½ teaspoon each cumin, chili powder and paprika
A few dashes of soy sauce
1 tablespoon lemon juice
A little liquid– I'd go with orange juice, broth or coconut milk
Breadcumbs
Oil for frying
Optional: add coconut to the preceding

Mix all but the breadcrumbs and frying oil and use enough flour/liquid to make it into firm balls. Chill. Make balls out of it (not too big), roll in breadcrumbs and fry until browned in some oil. Drain on absorbent paper, serve with mustard and relish.

1 teaspoon curry powder
1 tablespoon lemon juice
$^1/_3$ cup mustard
2 tablespoon grated onion
2 tablespoon minced dried apricots
1 tablespoon sesame oil
2 or 3 tablespoon water or apricot juice

Mix this all together. Add a little sugar, salt and pepper, chili powder if you wish.

The relish is easy, mix your favorite relish with extra minced onion, parsley, cilantro, a little mustard seed, and some minced chilies.

Spicy Okra with Sweet Tomatoes

2 lbs. sliced okra
2 lbs. chopped, drained sweet tomatoes
Mix of sweet and hot peppers, several of both, chopped
2 diced onions
1 tablespoon garam masala
2 teaspoon madras curry powder
Several tablespoon rice vinegar
½ cup chopped cilantro
2 tablespoon minced ginger
½ cup orange or pineapple juice
2 tablespoon lime juice
Peanut oil to fry
1 teaspoon mustard seeds
1 bay leaf
½ teaspoon ground cloves
A little tamarind paste or tomato paste
Salt and pepper

Begin frying okra, onions, mustard seeds and bay leaf with some salt and pepper in a few tablespoon peanut oil (or other oil). After 2–3 minutes add half of the garam masala and curry powder and the chilies. Stir and cook for several minutes more, then add tamarind paste, tomatoes, lime juice, cloves and ginger and cook for a couple of minutes. Add orange juice and the rest of the spice and half of the cilantro. Cook for 10 minutes, add more juice or some water as needed and a little rice vinegar to sharpen/sweeten it up if you need to, and cook for however much longer you feel like it. Adjust seasonings before you decide it's all finished. Served with some seasoned rice. It's good as a side or a second main dish. Use the rest of the cilantro as a garnish/fresh shot.

CINNAMON-CASHEW "CHICKEN" WITH FRIED VEGETABLES

2 teaspoon cinnamon
1 teaspoon five-spice
2 teaspoon red curry powder
½ teaspoon mustard seed
½ teaspoon each cumin and coriander seed
½ teaspoon fennel seed
1 curry leaf or lime leaf
A few tablespoon sugar or rice syrup
¼ cup sesame and peanut oil mixed (more if needed)
¼ cup soy sauce
2 tablespoon rice vinegar
1 small chopped onion
1 cup chopped roasted cashews
1 tablespoon sesame seeds
½ cup chopped cilantro
¼ cup chopped Thai basil
1 teaspoon minced lemongrass
4 cloved minced garlic
2 teaspoon minced ginger
2 teaspoon minced galangal
4 good-sized cutlets of veggie "chicken"/seitan/tempeh
2 cups cooked red rice

In a large pan, cook half each of the ingredients thru chicken (cook all of the chicken) until the cutlets are browned, then add the rice and the rest and cook until heated.

Sauté these vegetables in a little oil and place on the side of each serving:
1 chopped red onion
1 diced eggplant
2 chopped carrots
A few minced hot chilies
2 diced bell peppers
½ cup chopped water chestnut/celery/other crunchies

Sprinkle the veggies with some tamari, hoisin sauce, chili sauce or garlic sauce depending on whether you want it sweet, salty, spicy or garlicky. Sprinkle the whole affair on the plates with a little cinnamon.

BAKED PAPAYA IN RICE WINE

1 papaya, cut in half, seeds removed
1 cup rice wine
2 tablespoon sugar
¼ cup soy sauce
1 tablespoon rice vinegar
1 diced onion
½ cup chopped basil
½ teaspoon cloves
2 teaspoon curry powder
1 teaspoon coriander
Some minced herbs, whatever you like
1 tablespoon minced ginger
½ cup chopped cilantro
A few tablespoon chili sauce
A few tablespoon peanut oil

Place half the rice wine and the papaya
halves, cut side up, in a baking dish or
casserole. Poke the papayas with a knife.
Mix half the herbs, cilantro and basil, and
the rest of the ingredients to together and
pour over the papaya. Bake at 375° for 45
minutes to an hour. Serve scoops of the
baked papaya, drizzled with a little of the
dressing and sprinkled with herbs, cilantro
and basil.

"Comrade, comrade!"

Slap!

"Oh where have you gone?"

Water splashes on my face!

"Comrade, comrade!"

Slap!

Brightest light ever shining into my eyes. Can see only shapes– worst hangover of all time. So groggy…

"Have you found it? No, of course not! Come on get up, get into the kitchen and show what you DO know– secrets only! Or do you still need convincing!?"

Must not show… must not help… can't end like this…

They prodded and poked and plied me with various tortures like crumb tea and meat candy, bad tastes and foul textures… too bitter and too sweet, too hot and too meat. Ugh! The beet cocktail, well I liked that and the recipe's here (along with not a few of their secrets). Finally I broke and showed them a few things (they beet it out of me). I couldn't take it anymore, but not without getting a few tips from them as well! I didn't tell them even a half of a percent of what I knew but it didn't matter– they stole all their knowledge and took credit for it anyway, so each scrap was like a bar of gold as far as they were concerned. Hey, quit hitting me in the legs with that thing, I'm trying to cook here! If you smack me on the head with that cucumber again, I'll I'll, well… If they get this recipe before me, Lord knows what they can do with it… mass control… mind manipulation… world domination… who knows? I don't even know what the damn thing is yet. Got to get out of here… and what's with this goofy kitchen? Where the hell am I? A submarine? (Tink, tonk, tink, tonk…) If I could just reach that… Oh crap, too late, here comes their commander…

"Oh comrade, comrade, what a waste, a shame to waste such talent but we can't let you live. We can't let you reach the recipe before us, to keep and use what we have shown you– or even to continue on after what you have shown us– what we have learned– you are simply too dangerous and we, not you, must possess it all, do svidaniya my friend!"

The lights go back off, smack! The next thing I remember is a whole lot of water, as they dumped my swaddled body in the sea, more chain than clank.

Drop drop drop…

Thunk!

At least their food wasn't all bad. Can't we all just get along?

…*and, scene!*

Cherry-Almond Shake

½ cup cherry juice
2 cups almond milk (or hazelnut)
Insides of 1 vanilla bean
A little grated nutmeg
¼ cup sugar
2 or 3 tablespoon cherry syrup
a pinch of cloves

Blend all of this together and freeze until
slushy, then blend again and serve. Makes 4.

Beetini
(or "savage Beeting")

Juice a beet!
Vodka
Bitters
Horseradish, caraway seeds or cumin seeds

If desired:
Salt
Bitter lemon
Ice
Pickled beet (can u find baby ones?)

In a shaker mix 2 parts vodka to 1 part
beet juice with a dash of bitters and some
ice, horseradish and seeds if you like. Juice
the rim with a little bitter lemon and salt it,
then strain the cocktail into these glasses
and add a spear of pickled beet.

STUFFED CABBAGE LEAVES WRAPPED IN PASTRY

Pie pastry (add a little more margarine and
½ teaspoon baking powder)
8 large cabbage leaves, lightly-steamed
1 cup cooked rice
2 tablespoon dried black currants
½ cup sautéed ground veggie "beef" with a
little soy sauce
1 chopped green bell pepper
2 minced cloves garlic
A little horseradish
Salt and pepper
Cumin, caraway, coriander, allspice
½ cup chopped red onion
2 tablespoon minced marjoram
⅓ cup chopped parsley
A little oil

Mix together cooked rice thru "a little oil"–
just use about 2 tablespoon of oil. Divide
pastry dough into 8 balls and roll them out.
Lay a cabbage leaf on each, stuff each leaf
with rice mixture (don't overfill it, you want
to fold still). Roll the cabbage leaf up and
fold the dough around it and crimp shut
however you please. Bake on lightly-greased
sheet (prick with a fork or score with a knife
and brush them lightly with oil or melted
margarine) at 400° for about 25 minutes.

A nice sauce for this– 1 cup vegan cream
cheese, 2 tablespoon lemon juice, ¼ cup dill,
3 garlic cloves, ¼ cup Dijon mustard, ¼ cup
white wine or vodka, and a healthy amount
of salt and pepper, some horseradish if you
like– puréed and warmed (a little similar to
the beet pancake sauce).

Kale and Potato Salad

2 lbs. potatoes, boiled and sliced
2 bunches of kale, chopped
1 white onion, thinly sliced
$1/3$ cup cider vinegar
A little sunflower oil
2 teaspoon sugar
Salt, pepper, coriander and cumin to taste
½ cup chopped flat-leaf parsley
½ cup chopped sweet red peppers
2 tablespoon capers

Sauté kale and half of the onion in oil with salt, pepper and spices until cooked (only takes about 10 minutes). You should put the cover on for half the time, sprinkling with a little cider vinegar before. Drain and mix with the other ingredients, adding more spice, salt and pepper to taste. Add the cider vinegar slowly as the full amount you may find off-putting (I don't!). Stop when it's delicious. Sprinkle with roasted sunflower seeds if you desire. Vegenaise or mustard may be added to the dressing but it's not necessary.

HAZELNUT-CHOCOLATE PUDDING WITH COFFEE "CREAM"

½ cup hazelnut syrup
½ cup Frangelico
1 cup melted chocolate
2 cups sugar
2 cups tofu cream cheese
1½ cup to 2 cups almond milk (you can use more if you want it to be thinner)
1 tablespoon cornstarch
1/3 cup flour
¼ cup oil or margarine
3 teaspoon vanilla
1 tablespoon instant coffee
Lemon juice
½ cup toasted or candied, chopped hazelnuts

Mix hazelnut syrup, Frangelico, 1½ cup sugar, melted chocolate, flour, cornstarch, almond milk, 1 cup vegan cream cheese, 2 teaspoon vanilla, margarine or oil and cook on the stovetop, stirring until it thickens a bit.

Chill.

Blend instant coffee, 1 cup tofu cream cheese, lemon juice, ½ cup sugar and 1 teaspoon vanilla and chill.

Serve these two layered in parfait glasses with candied hazelnuts on top.

BEET PANCAKES WITH CREAMY DILL SAUCE AND WILD MUSHROOM-WALNUT SPREAD

2 lbs. grated or diced beets
1 sliced onion
2 diced carrots
1 teaspoon each cumin, coriander, paprika
1 teaspoon caraway seed
Salt and pepper
2 tablespoon red wine vinegar
At least 1 cup flour
1 teaspoon baking powder
1 tablespoon sugar
2 tablespoon mustard
1 tablespoon grated horseradish
2 tablespoon each minced dill, marjoram, parsley

Mix it all together to make nice pancake batter, adding more liquid or flour as needed. Fry ¼ cup or $^1/_3$ cup dollops of batter in light oil, turning once, until browned/cooked on both sides, serve with the yummy sauces.

½ cup tofu cream cheese
¼ cup chopped dill
$^1/_3$ cup unflavored soy milk/creamer
2 crushed garlic cloves
2 tablespoon grated onion
2 tablespoon olive oil
Lemon juice to taste
Salt and pepper

Blend until smooth, serve with pancakes.
2 cups chopped wild mushrooms
soy sauce to taste
1 cup chopped walnuts

A few tablespoon olive oil
1 diced onion
Salt, pepper and paprika
A few tablespoon chopped marjoram
1 minced bell pepper (probably use red but it doesn't matter too much)
1 or 2 tablespoon balsamic vinegar

Sauté mushrooms and walnuts with half of the onion, salt, pepper, marjoram and paprika in the oil until the mushrooms start to shrink down a little. Add vinegar, bell pepper and the rest of the onion and some parsley and serve warm or chilled with the pancakes.

POTATO POCKETS WITH CARROT SALSA AND SWEET AND SOUR BEET GLAZE

Pastry dough (add 1 teaspoon baking powder, maybe a little more liquid and some onion powder)
2 cups cooked potatoes, mashed
½ cup vegan cream cheese
Salt and pepper
2 tablespoon margarine
½ cup chopped onion
¼ cup chopped parsley
1 teaspoon paprika
2 tablespoon prepared mustard
1 tablespoon lemon juice
2 tablespoon minced herbs (dill, marjoram, etc.)
Optional: a tablespoon of nutritional yeast helps

Mix all but pastry dough together. Roll small balls of dough out fairly thinly, stuff with 2 or 3 tablespoon of the potato mixture, fold over and crimp the edge. You can bake them on a greased sheet with a light baste of oil at 400° for 22 minutes, or fry them in a pan until golden brown on both sides and serve with the accompaniments.

2 cups chopped carrots
½ teaspoon mustard seeds
1 tablespoon capers
hot and bell peppers, chopped small
2 tablespoon olive oil/sunflower oil
2 tablespoon toasted sunflower seeds
½ teaspoon each cumin and coriander seed
Salt and pepper to taste
¼ cup minced red onion
Red wine vinegar to taste
½ cup chopped parsely
½ teaspoon red chili flakes

Mix this together for "salsa".

½ cup cooked beets
¼ cup lemon juice
2 tablespoon red wine vinegar
¼ cup sugar
½ teaspoon cornstarch
½ cup water or broth or orange juice
Pinch of cumin or coriander, salt to taste

Liquefy this and simmer in a saucepan, stirring, until it thickens a bit– about 20 minutes.

STRING BEAN, VEGGIE FISH, PARSNIPS AND HERBS IN GOLDEN GARLIC-ONION BROTH

8 cups golden broth (add more bouillon cubes if the broth isn't tasty enough)– use more for a thinner soup
3 diced onions
Several garlic cloves, sliced plus 4 more minced cloves (have extra on hand)
2–3 tablespoon olive oil plus a little more for frying
3 diced carrots
2 lbs. chopped green beans
2 lbs. chopped parsnips
1 lb. diced sweet potatoes
2 lbs. chopped potatoes
Salt and pepper
1½ teaspoon paprika
¼ cup each chopped parsley, thyme, rosemary, sage and marjoram
2 or 3 bay leaves
½ teaspoon each cumin seed, allspice, celery seed, crushed coriander
2 red bell peppers, thinly sliced
tempeh, tofu or other fake meat
Sushi nori
A little garlic olive oil
Some minced garlic chives

Soak the fake meat in soy sauce, maybe a little chili sauce and some balsamic vinegar, some of the paprika and some minced garlic and onions with olive or sesame oil for a while, wrap tightly in strips of nori and set aside.

Sauté the rest of the minced garlic in olive oil and set aside.

Bring to a boil veggie broth, garlic and sautéed garlic (with the oil), spices, bay leaves, half of the carrots, potatoes, parsnips, half of the herbs and half of the onions. Lower to a simmer and cook for 15–20 minutes. Add sweet potatoes, green beans, and the rest of the herbs, onion and carrots and cook for another 10–15 minutes. Stir in red pepper slices just as you turn the heat off.

At the very end, slice the "fishy strips" and place them on the soup serving. Drizzle with a little garlic olive oil and sprinkle with garlic chives.

Potato-Cucumber Salad with onions and Sweet-Sour Parsley Vinaigrette

2 or 3 lbs. potatoes, cut into slices
1 thinly sliced onion
2 cucumbers, stripe-peeled and sliced
A handful of chopped parsley
1 tablespoon sugar
¼ cup vinegar
2 or 3 tablespoon oil
½ teaspoon ground coriander
½ teaspoon whole crushed cumin seeds
½ teaspoon celery seed
2 tablespoon capers
A couple of shakes of paprika
Salt and pepper
Additions: Add caraway if you like, or
mustard

Boil potatoes until cooked but still a little
firm. Drain and then mix with the other
ingredients and chill.

Boy was I lucky! A large kelp bubble just happened to attach to my face on the way down– whew! That was a close one! But I'm not out of the sinewy woods yet am I? Who are these clowns, pitchforks– tails! I must have died after all… what the? Hey, hands off, hey I'd rather drown than go with you types– hey! Alright, alright already quit with the pushing and the poking. I'm coming, I'm coming!

Oh geez, I had this all wrong. They put me in an air-filled room walled with some kind of strong glass and sealed the door. A great echoing warbly underwater fanfare commenced and with the biggest hoopla a curtain in front of me parted and there on a throne sat a great blue bastard with a crown, fins and a tail, glorious robes, trident and the ugliest mug you've ever seen.

"No, I'm not Poseidon, you fool, I can read your thoughts. Just a mer-king of cookery! We know of your quest and certainly will do all we can to help you on your journey. But before you go, you must help *us* with a few problems down here."

Such as…

"Such as? Such insolence! Such as we still haven't figured out what to do with this!" He held up some tangled glistening sea mess. Oh brother, here we go again!

Well, I'm game, and here's some approximations of what we managed to do, although, frankly, some of it was so disgusting it is best not to be replicated, remade or even mimicked or described!

Plus you couldn't even touch what they were doing down there– they rode around on seahorses corralling weird sea critters. They farmed vast fields of sea vegetables (underwater factory farms!) and had crazy huge "open water" markets every Saturday at the palace steps where you could swim over and buy most any ocean delight or sunken treasure your heart desired. I never really figured out their barter system. I came in with shells and wound up with Manhattan (or rather the opposite).

Whenever I went out, I had a diver's suit equipped with an airtank and helmet. Whenever they came in they wore a seaweed suit and helmet full of water. Takes all kinds. We cooked sometimes in my room's normal kitchen, or…

Their fire was a volcanic underwater fissure and they cooked there greedily. Can't smell a thing! Didn't we all have a hell of a time– all in all, an interesting place to visit but I wouldn't want to live there!

After a lot of jealous coveting of my skills, they finally sent me on my way, through what they claimed was a "short cut".

"Speed on your journey, the rotund ones of the centre shall greet you and show you on your way", they exclaimed, as they shoved me into some weird hole, which turned into a cave, which turned into a road. Hey, "dry land" at last, albeit a bit strange. I'm in the damn rock! No sun, no sky, rotunds? Well, whatever. At least I was on my way!

miso mary

For two:
8 oz. tomato or vegetable juice
1 carrot
½ teaspoon miso paste
1 teaspoon ginger (fresh!)
A little wasabi (your call on this)
2 tablespoon chopped daikon radish
2 tablespoon lemon juice
4 oz. vodka (more to taste)
I would rock a small dash of dry vermouth
on this
Mixed black peppercorns in a grinder with
crumbled dry seaweed (nori works fine,
something not sticky)
Spears or pickles: asparagus, daikon, ginger,
shiso leaf if you like

Blend ingredients up to/including lemon
juice. Strain over ice. Add vodka and a little
vermouth. Sprinkle with a few turns of
the pepper-seaweed mixture and decorate
with pickles and veggie spears.

MANGO, AVOCADO, WATERCRESS, SEAWEED DRESSING

2 peeled mangoes, sliced into strips
2 avocados, cut into pieces
2 bunches chopped watercress
¼ cup seaweed, reconstituted and chopped,
your choice
Several tablespoon plum or rice vinegar
1 teaspoon toasted rice, ground to powder
with a little salt
2–3 tablespoon mustard oil or other
amusing oil
Salt and pepper to taste
1 tablespoon miso
Optional: add ginger, daikon, red bell
peppers, pineapple or some other fun stuff

Place the first three ingredients in a bowl.
Mix the others and add to your salad. All set!

VEG. "FISH" TEMPURA

A pack or two of sushi nori, cut into strips–
teriyaki or other flavor may be nice (you
can also use other seaweeds for the wraps,
particularly wakame)
1 lb. tempeh, cut into strips and marinated
in soy sauce, chili sauce, sesame oil and
vinegar overnight
1 lb. sweet potato, cut into substantial
pieces (cooked but still firmish)
1 lb. taro root, cut into thick strips (again
cooked but not falling apart)
1 lb. baked seasoned tofu, cut into squares
soy sauce
A few tablespoon black vinegar/rice
vinegar
Sesame oil, sesame seeds
Chili sauce
Minced garlic
Minced onion
Wasabi
Ginger
Coriander
Mustard or mustard seeds

This is very easy. What you do is season
the sweet potato, tempeh, taro root and
baked tofu well and allow them to sit for a
little bit, using combinations of the other
ingredients. Try to make each taste a little
different. Roll the pieces up in strips of
seaweed, then dip them in this batter…

Batter:
½ cup flour
½ cup rice flour
1 teaspoon baking powder
$^2/_3$ cup soda water/beer (more for thinner
batter if you like)
Salt and pepper to taste
I like a little garlic or onion powder in this,
a little seaweed flake and some toasted
ground sesame seeds
Oil for frying

Dip the little fishies in the batter and fry
until golden. Serve with a vast array of
condiments, maybe vegan lumpia sauce
would be good or one of those odd little
vegan "fish" sauces. By the end of the book
you should have a good handle on how
to make things more "fishy" tasting if you
really want to.

Seaweed salad is good with this– 1
cup chopped wakame, a little onion or
scallion, a small bit of ginger, 2 tablespoon
seasoned rice vinegar, 2 teaspoon soy
sauce, 1 tablespoon toasted sesame seeds
and a drizzle of sesame oil.

BAKED VEGGIE "FISH" WITH LEMON SAUCE, CUCUMBER CHUTNEY AND JICAMA-TARO ROOT MEDLEY

1 lb. veggie "meat"/tempeh or seasoned tofu, cut into four cutlets
Season this with:
2 tablespoon plum vinegar
1 tablespoon olive oil
3 minced cloves garlic
½ cup minced onion
1 teaspoon each garlic powder, turmeric, celery seed
2 tablespoon prepared mustard
Several tablespoon soy sauce
Next, wrap these in some…

Sushi nori or other seaweed that can wrap

And dip them in a batter of…

½ cup Flour
Salt and pepper to taste
½ cup Rice flour
$^1/_3$ cup Beer (more for a thinner batter)
½ teaspoon baking soda
1 tablespoon olive oil

Place in a greased baking dish arrayed with lemon slices and bake at 400° for 30 or 40 minutes, turning once (until browned). When you turn it, I would sprinkle some seaweed-seasoned breadcrumbs on top. Essentially it is like veg. fish inside of a baked pancake.

½ cup Lemon juice
½ cup shredded, seeded Lemons
$^1/_3$ cup sugar
Rice wine to taste
½ cup broth
1 teaspoon cornstarch (a little more for thicker)
1 teaspoon ground toasted sesame seeds
Salt and white pepper to taste
¼ cup minced or grated onion
2 minced or pressed garlic cloves
1 teaspoon grated ginger
1 tablespoon prepared mustard
I would throw in a teaspoon or so of seasoning mix as well, like Spike or something

This is the sauce, mix together and whisk/stir over medium heat until it begins to thicken. Season to your liking, in particular it probably needs more sugar.

1 cup chopped cucumber
½ teaspoon radish seed or celery seed
2 teaspoon sugar
2 minced spicy peppers
1 tablespoon vinegar
½ cup diced onion
1 diced carrot
1 or 2 teaspoon green curry paste
½ cup cilantro and basil
Pinch of cardamom
A little oil

Here's your relish, mix together and re-season, it is really not necessary to cook it.

1 cup cooked diced taro root
1 cup diced jicama
¼ cup minced cilantro
½ cup chopped bell pepper (green and red)
1 or 2 diced avocados
1 teaspoon minced ginger
2 minced garlic cloves
Salt and pepper to taste
2 tablespoon grated onion
1 tablespoon lemon juice
A little seaweed seasoning mix (your favorite)
1 tablespoon oil (more if needed)
Plum vinegar to taste
A few tablespoon of vegan mayonnaise
A little prepared mustard
Mix, season and serve room temperature or chilled with the rest.

VEGGIE FRIED "FISH" IN SPICY GREEN SAUCE

1 lb. tempeh or baked tofu, cut into strips
Sushi nori
A little oil for frying
Soy sauce, chili sauce, curry and such to
marinate the tempeh

Marinate the tempeh in some soy sauce,
chili sauce, curry paste (a little), maybe some
vinegar or whatever else for a few hours,
turning every now and again. Take them
out and roll each strip in a strip of seaweed,
tightly. Allow to sit for a few minutes and then
fry in modest amounts of oil, turning once,
until browned on both sides. Serve with this
green sauce and some seasoned rice with a
nice dash of seaweed seasoning mix.

½ cup minced hot chilies
1 chopped Onion
2 tablespoon rice vinegar
¼ cup oil
¼ cup capers
¼ cup chopped parsley
¼ cup chopped cilantro
¼ cup chopped basil
1 or 2 tablespoon crushed pickled green
peppercorns
Lime juice to taste

Mix these together and add salt and
pepper/seasoning to taste. You can simmer
it for a few minutes/purée it or whatever
or just serve it as is with your veggie num
nums.

Fried Veg. "Fish" Cubes with Onion, Peppers, Carrots and Zucchini in Herb and Cumin Sauce with Olive-Cous Cous, Parsley and Artichoke Heart Pilaf, Roasted Beets with Green Beans and Nectarine Relish

2 eggplants (cube and then coat with salt, pepper, olive oil, lemon juice and seaweed flakes)
1 chopped onion
3 minced garlic clove
2 bell peppers, chopped (add some spicy ones too if you like)
2 diced carrots
2 half-moon sliced zucchini
1 teaspoon cumin seed
veggie broth (as needed)
½ cup flat-leafed parsley
¼ cup chopped marjoram
¼ cup soy sauce
Salt, pepper, paprika, chili flakes to taste
Flour (enough to dredge)
A little mustard or tahini if desired
Oil for frying

Heat oil in a large skillet. Dredge eggplant in some seasoned flour and begin frying them with the onions and garlic and cumin seeds. After a few minutes add the rest of the vegetables, some seasonings, and the herbs and cook until zucchini is tender. Add a little broth to make sauce and season again, add a little mustard or tahini sauce to make it more interesting.

Serve with cous cous.

1½ to 2 cups cous cous
1 cup mixed chopped olives
½ cup parsley
1 chopped red bell pepper
2 cups artichoke hearts
3 cloves minced garlic
1 chopped onion
2 lbs. beets
½ cup toasted pine nuts or chopped toasted hazelnuts

Trim and peel beets and dice them. Place in a baking dish with a little water, oil, salt and pepper– just enough to coat. Roast at 375° for 35–40 minutes, turning once and slathering with a little more liquid if necessary. Time the cous cous to coincide with them being done.

Prepare couscous according to the laws of cous cous. Meanwhile, sauté artichoke hearts, onion, garlic in olive oil with some of the spice until they start to brown. When everything is done mix it all together with cous cous, salt and pepper to taste and the rest of the herbs and spices. A side of sautéed green beans or as an addition to the cous cous is great.

2 seeded chopped nectarines
1 tablespoon minced ginger
1 tablespoon lemon juice
2 tablespoon grated red onion
1 teaspoon toasted sesame seeds
¼ cup chopped parsley
A little sugar
Pinch of sumac
A few pinches of cardamom
A little cinnamon

½ teaspoon cumin
½ teaspoon coriander
¼ cup nectarine juice
2 tablespoon olive oil
A little marmelade

Mix this together and serve as a side relish.

Ah, I think I'm finally getting acclimated to this place– the air doesn't seem quite so stuffy. The light is changing, from that scary fire red into purple, then how about this nice blue glow, and ah... emerald green. Hunh... I think I hear something... What's that smell? Not sulphur this time, thank goodness! Yummm, dumplings? It can't be! And that pounding– what is all the ruckus about?

Thump thump!

Is that chanting too? Something's coming! I'd better hide.

"RO-tund! RO-tund! Roley-Poley, PO-Tund!"

Thump! Thump! Pound pound! Dun dun DAH! Dum DUM!

Hey this is what I call a greeting! A bunch of round, happy trolls with a marching band, chanting and bearing all sorts of little round cakes, pies, croquettes and dumplings just for me! For me? Oh really you shouldn't have. I guess I can come out from behind this giant incandescent mushroom now.

Oh and who's this great big one? Must be the leader.

"Roley Poley, welcome to the centre, Sir Journey Roll! Oh we hear from the Mer-King of your quest and shall take you through the secret passage to the Crusty Cavern near the surface. But first, we have heard that you, Sir Roll, are a fine cook and perhaps to help 'round out our rounds, ball up our balls, find and fill the creamy centres with all manner of delights, put our spheres in good cheer and generally roll up our roley-poley sleeves, Sir Roll, that we Rotunds may from hither on be more Well-Rounded."

Yes of course, Your Rolliness.

"Excellent, excellent! Let us roll for a stroll, Sir Roll, and speak in circles of this curvaceous cuisine!"

And so it went, yet again. Needless to say, they ate only things that were round or made to be round in their round little ovens in their round little homes and popped them like gumballs into their round mouths to fill their round roley-poly little bodies (recipes follow). And everything that grew, whether cucumber, carrot, celery or creature– was strangely, suspiciously round. Isn't there any NATURAL food anywhere anymore? First the aqua-ag and now this... Oh well, c'est la guerre!

I finally asked why they kept calling me a roll instead of a round. To which it was replied, "Bcuz, Sir Roll, thou art long and not rotund, yet still possessed of a circumference– perhaps like your ah Bbuuhrrrrrito or Toooohtseee Rrrrrohlllluh..." Ah well, that makes sense!

I almost hated to leave, especially when with a great RO-tund "rum-PUM-PUM!", they marched me to the edge of the great, vast, foul, nasty, crumb strewn, Crusty Cavern. As the din of their colossal round drums faded into the background, I made my way haltingly, cautiously through the brambles, old furniture, scraps of fabric, branches, weeds and spare-changers...ever on, dreading what strange bug or beast might next approach, when I began to hear a thin music as from a harp, and the light finally began to glow as the regular sun...

roly poly melon boly

Honeydew melon
¼ cup Midori
½ cup rum
A few cups passion fruit punch or guava
juice
Little round gummies (put them in there
if you like)
Soda water
Limes, cut into wedges

What a great green glob! I loved this drink.
Simply cut the top off the melon and
scoop out the goop and seeds. Then take
out some of the melon flesh and blend
with this other stuff (except soda water
and lime wedges) and pour it into the
melon, finishing with soda water and a
few lime wedges. Cut a hole in the top for
a straw, and then put the top back on the
melon and set it in a bowl, drink out of it
with a nice curly, curvaceous straw!

ITSY BITSY "MEATBALL" AND DUMPLING SOUP

1 lb. veggie "ground beef" log
1½ cup flour
1 packet dry active yeast
1 teaspoon baking powder
Oil
Salt and pepper
8 cups broth
2 chopped onions (actually mince half of one for your "meatballs")
3 minced garlic cloves
2 teaspoon tomato paste
½ cup chopped mixed herbs
1 bay leaf
1 teaspoon each chili powder, cumin, celery seed
2 diced carrots
2 chopped green peppers
Additions: maybe throw some turnips or something in there, chopped kale, whatever veggie you want, add some sherry to the broth

Activate dry yeast in $^1/_3$ cup warm water. Add 1¼ cup flour, baking powder, plus salt to taste and a drizzle of oil. Also, optionally add a teaspoon each of paprika and curry powder. Mix together and add more liquid if you need to to make a soft, easily workable dough.

Allow to rise for an hour, then punch it down and knead it and start your soup. Bring to a boil the broth, herbs, garlic, bay leaf, carrots, salt and pepper to taste, chopped onions, and whatever else you wish. Allow to simmer for 10 minutes or so, then form the dough into little balls and drop into the broth. Add the green peppers. Bring to a boil again and then simmer these for 10–15 minutes and the soup is done.

Whilstwhile, form your "meat log" into little balls by mixing with some flour (¼ cup), tomato paste, soy sauce and minced onions, plus some pepper and a little nutmeg. Fry them up in some olive oil until browned.

Add to the soup at the end or place them in the bowl for each serving.

A small seedless grape or a caper may be placed in the center of each "meatball" and a green olive in the center of each dumpling if you like, that's what they did!

magic egg

Here's a weird one, it wasn't even Easter!

(Don't forget to have food coloring, coconut, and frying oil on hand and some little chocolate eggs as well)

2 cups flour (reserve some for rolling)
½ cup vanilla soy milk (warm)
$^1/_3$ cup coconut milk
½ teaspoon to 1 teaspoon salt
½ cup sugar
2 teaspoon baking powder
1 pkg. dry active yeast

Mix yeast, sugar and warm soy milk and allow to sit for 5 minutes. Mix in the rest to make a nice dough. Allow to rise/sit for an hour. Then roll out balls to ¼ inch thick rounds. And stuff each with two mixtures...

One...
½ cup tofu cream cheese
½ teaspoon vanilla
2 teaspoon lemon juice
2 teaspoon flour
¼ cup sugar

Two...
½ cup of your favorite jelly
Mixed with a little cinnamon sugar
And 1 teaspoon grated ginger

To do this, place a dollop of one on one end of the dough, and a dollop of the other on the other end. Roll up in such fashion that the two globs are contained each within their own chamber inside the dough (you'll figure it out, I do this instead of piping it in because I prefer the hot "cream cheese" for this one!). Now form the thing back into a ball or "egg" shape. Roll in some grated coconut. Fry in Hot oil, turning, until golden brown. It shouldn't unwrap if you were careful. Sprinkle with colored coconut (may I suggest green, pink or something garish). A little powdered sugar and nutmeg spruces it up as well.

(Feeling ambitious? Put a chocolate egg in the center of each of 'em!)

To truly present this, you need to lay the "eggs" in a bed of colored coconut "grass", and all about strew little chocolate eggs or balls, as well as some vegan cream cheese and sugar balls rolled in yet more coconut. Then drizzle the whole thing with chocolate sauce. And also how about a "white chocolate" sauce dyed pink or blue or something.

FRIED ZUCCHINI LOGS STUFFED WITH OLIVE "CREAM CHEESE"

Several zucchini, cut into round logs
1 cup seasoned herb bread crumbs mixed with a few tablespoon flour
Olive oil
1 cup tofu cream cheese
2 tablespoon lemon juice
Salt and pepper
½ teaspoon each paprika and chili powder (plus some to sprinkle)
2 or 3 minced garlic cloves
1 minced onion
½ cup chopped herbs
1 cup chopped mixed olives
¼ cup chopped flat leaf parsley
Oil for frying

Mix together vegan cream cheese, onion, herbs and parsley, spices, a little olive oil, olives, salt and pepper, garlic and lemon juice and chill. Core out the centers of your zucchini logs and sprinkle with a little salt and lemon juice, and score the outsides of the logs lengthwise. Stuff each with some of the vegan cream cheese-olive mixture, then roll the logs first in a little olive oil and then in the flour-seasoned breadcrumb mix. Next fry them in a modest amount of oil, turning, until browned. Or, mayhaps, you can bake the little buggers at 400° for 30 minutes or so, turning once. Serve with marinara sauce, pesto dip, roasted pepper hummous, tahini dressing or something awesome like that.

"CREAM CHEESE" AND "SALAMI" STUFFED BREADED AND DEEP FRIED OLIVES WITH AIOLI

Some big-ass pitted olives
½ cup melted margarine or olive oil
2 teaspoon cornstarch
1 teaspoon baking powder
1 cup flour
1 cup seasoned Italian breadcrumbs
Salt and pepper
Garlic (how about 6 to 8 cloves)
$^1/_3$ cup minced onion
½ cup chopped veggie "salami"
Tofu cream cheese
Lemon juice (oh… how about half a cup-half for the batter and half for the sauce?)
A little minced oregano
¼ cup olive oil for the sauce
Oil for frying
Capers

Mix veg, cream cheese, chopped "salami", 2 minced garlic cloves, oregano, onion, 1 teaspoon lemon juice, a little parsley and salt and pepper to taste. Stuff each olive with this mixture, try to get one caper into the middle of each (if you wanted to cannibalize, add chopped olives to it, ha ha!). Mix together flour, baking powder, a little salt, garlic powder. Keep that in one bowl. In another mix lemon juice, corn starch and margarine/oil. Dip olives in the flour, then the oil mixture, then the flour again, then quickly in the oil, then in the breadcrumbs. Seems like a messy pain in the ass but I thought I'd make it annoying for you (fun with friends!). And do try to do the whole procedure quickly.

Fry the little buggers in oil until browned, it doesn't have to be deep fried. You can also bake them.

Now blend the rest of the garlic, olive oil and lemon juice until smooth, adding a little salt and pepper to taste. Jazz it up with some pomegranate concentrate and a little sugar.

Deep Fried Blueberry "Steak" Balls

2 cups chopped veggie "steak" strips
½ cup smashed blueberries
½ cup minced onions
2 minced garlic cloves
Couple tablespoon sugar
A few tablespoon of your favorite steak sauce
1 teaspoon each chili powder, cumin, onion powder
At least a cup of flour
½ cup chopped herbs (rosemary is good in this, also thyme, sage, parsley, dill)
1 teaspoon or a little more baking powder
Salt and pepper, soy sauce to taste
½ teaspoon ground allspice
½ teaspoon to 1 teaspoon cinnamon (as you like)

Add some mustard to the batter if you like beer as needed to make nice the balls, or other liquid with a little soda water (How about blueberry juice or blueberry beer?!)
Seasoned breadcrumbs, in this case ground up cornflakes might be pretty sexy
Oil for frying

Mix all that together except the frying oil and breadcrumbs, adding more or less flour or beer as needed. Chill, then form into balls and roll in the breadcrumbs. Fry in liberal oil, turning as needed, until browned. Serve with mustard and British steak sauce (you know, the kind with the tamarind in it).

They like to put a big blueberry encased in vegan cream cheese right in the middle of each ball– they crazy!

CURRIED "CHICKEN" DUMPLINGS WITH ORANGE TOMATO CHUTNEY AND PEANUT BUTTER-WASABI SAUCE

1^1/$_3$ cup flour
½ cup chickpea flour
¾ cup warm water (more if needed)
½ to teaspoon salt (whatever you prefer)
1 teaspoon curry powder
1 teaspoon baking powder
1 pkg. dry active yeast
1 tablespoon sugar
2 tablespoon oil (a little sesame perhaps)

Activate yeast with warm water and sugar. Add the rest and mix to form a dough. It should be soft but not sticky. Set aside to rise for about an hour.

1 lb. shredded veggie chicken (or other)
½ cup chopped onions (add some green onions to jazz it up)
3 cloves minced garlic
1/3 cup peas
1 diced carrot
a little chopped cilantro
2 tablespoon tamarind sauce
1 tablespoon chili-garlic sauce
2 tablespoon oil
2 teaspoon curry powder
½ teaspoon garam masala
½ teaspoon crushed mustard seeds
Pepper to taste
Soy sauce to taste
Lemon juice to taste

Mix this together and set aside. Now take little pieces of dough and roll them out. Fill with a tablespoon or two of the chikn mixture

and seal tightly. Form into little buns. Cook them in a steamer for 20-25 minutes or until the dough is done to your liking. Seam/close (hole-side up in case they start to open while steaming– you don't want the stuff spilling out).

2 oranges, seeded, peeled and chopped
2 small tomatoes, chopped and drained
1 or 2 tablespoon vinegar
½ teaspoon ground cardamom
½ teaspoon pickling spice
1 teaspoon garam masala
1 diced onion
2 tablespoon sugar
1 or 2 tablespoon oil
salt and pepper to taste
2 teaspoon chili sauce
1 tablespoon prepared mustard
¼ cup orange juice

Heat all of this to a simmer, for 5 to 10 minutes, then allow to cool, now add: more spice!, ¼ cup chopped cilantro, some diced red onion, a little grated carrot, salt and sugar to taste, some fresh minced red chili, and a bit of lime and orange juice. About a teaspoon of grated orange peel is nice as well.

2 tablespoon prepared wasabi
2 tablespoon rice vinegar
¼ cup peanut butter
1 teaspoon grated ginger
1 or 2 minced garlic cloves
Soy sauce to taste
¼ cup broth (more for a thinner sauce)
A little lemon juice

Mix this together and season to taste. Allow to sit a bit before serving.

Tomato Boats stuffed with Curried "Chicken" Salad

1 cup chopped veggie chicken (more to stuff the toms higher)
A few tablespoon soy sauce
A few tablespoon each minced sage, dill, parsley, marjoram (have a little extra parsley handy)
1 chopped onion
1 tablespoon curry powder
½ teaspoon each ground cumin and coriander
2–3 tablespoon lemon juice
2–3 tablespoon capers
2–3 tablespoon mustard
1 or 2 minced red/orange bell peppers
½ cup chopped green olives
Some olive oil
6 roma tomatoes
Salt and pepper
Paprika to sprinkle

Cut the tomatoes in half and scoop out the insides. Sprinkle with a little salt and pepper and allow to drain in a colander. Sauté the onion and veggie chicken with peppers, half of the herbs, half of the curry powder, the cumin and coriander and the soy sauce in some olive oil until the "chicken" starts to brown. Remove from heat and add everything else (not the tomato halves– der!). Fill each tomato half with this junk and then sprinkle with parsley and paprika and chill thems. If the filling is too dry, add some mustard, lemon juice and/or olive oil to it.

FRIED CHICKPEAS *with* GREENS, HERBS, TOMATOES *and* "FARMER'S CHEESE" BALLS ROLLED IN PARSLEY-GARLIC FLAKES

3 or 4 tomatoes, cut into wedges
A head or two of salad greens (let's say arugula and spinach for argument's sake)
2 tablespoon each minced herbs: sage, basil, oregano, etc. (pick three or four)
1 cup tofu cream cheese (chilled)
2–3 tablespoon lemon juice
Sea salt
1 cup minced parsley
¼ cup dried garlic flakes
1 cup cooked chickpeas
1 teaspoon chili powder
Salt and pepper
Oil for frying
A few tablespoon balsamic vinegar
A few tablespoon olive oil
Variations: olives, sliced cucumber, roasted pepper slices, artichoke hearts, radishes– any of these can be added

Stir 2 tablespoon lemon juice and a little salt into chilled vegan cream cheese. Form into little balls and roll in a mix of the parsley and garlic flakes. Chill these to keep firm.

Fry the chickpeas in some oil until they start to brown and then accost them with some salt and chili powder. Allow to cool a bit.

Compose a salad of the rest. Add your favorite salad dressing if you like, to send it over the top. And then go crazy– toss in the seasoned fried chickpeas and then array the little cheeseballs all about. Ta-da!

Suddenly I was amongst a bunch of palms and strangely coloured bird of paradise. How long had I been walking through this instead of the crusty pile? I hadn't even noticed. I suddenly felt very peaceful and wanted to spell everything with a 'u' like "colour" and "flavour".

Harp music listed along on the breeze and soon a great troop of curly-locked gods and goddesses adorned with gold and gems and swathed in rich purple and white scarves and cloaks, came effortlessly lilting through the leaves upon pillow-piled luxurious litters.

"Ah, ah, tee-hee ah, ah, roo coo coo", they tittled. "So pleased, Soul, to find you here, weren't thou lost? Oh, INDEED, wait, inDEED thou art not lost. Ah, the rotunds, bless their dear little round-souled hearts. The rotunds, they are simply adorable. They have kindly sent word of your arrival and of your little bitty cute little mission as well... How simply de-e-elightful!" They all applauded, "yes yes, in-DEED, in-DEED, how precious!

"But even though wishing we not to impose upon thee and thy little adventure, so precious, my friend dear Soul, wouldst thou not tarry a bit rather than harry a bit?"

Uh, sure.

"It is indeed ever so long since our most recent visitor graced us with the presence of another Soul, and we DO so enjoy the delights of comfort and companie!"

Yeah, whatever floats your boat, Princess.

"Oooh, goodie! Huzzah huzzah! Play now the harps and fyfe tee-tee-tee. And perhaps some sinfully rapacious cookery, in this we might also engage in harmony? N'est-ce pas?"

Oh, yes, of course, of course.

"Indeed! Onward, my merrie companions, onward!".

And on we went to their gold and silk inlaid huts, very comfortable they made efficient use of the space they had and the quaint little homes seemed more like palaces. Like everyone lived in the 'mother-in-law' in back of Versailles.

They did me up in luxurious scarves and festooned me with baubles and jewels, plied me with herbal and scented liqueurs and tasty, mildly sweet treats. Harps were always playing as if weaving a spell, and they were always eating and drinking and feasting and playing games and chattering in their erudite chatter and they clapped about nearly everything and squealed in delighted tizzies at nearly every pleasing development. They would roll down and wallow about the roads, which were covered in decadent fabrics instead of paved, and their cooking was quite divine and refined. In fact...

Everything they did was a bit effete, almost too refined to my taste. You could get lost here, no wonder they never go anywhere! Even though they had the freshest, best water I've ever tasted, they always filled each pitcher and glass with herbs, fruits, plump vegetables and jewels, drinking it, cooking with it, even bathing in it! Seconds turned to minutes to hours to days. It was always the same glowing light–time and I believe they themselves never slept but rather lazed-about all the time. With the occasional unfinished game of croquet or lawn darts as the only physical activity besides feasting, harp playing and backgammon (doesn't anyone ride a bike around here? I guess you can't really ride on fabric!). And they never explained who they were–Atlanteans perhaps? They certainly were advanced, if a bit bored/boring.

It was too easy to cook there, and frankly, they really didn't need my help. I think they just wanted the company.

After even days or what could have been years I finally got tired of the plush pillows and upholstered roads, and that dratted twanging harp music. Could you maybe, oh I dunno, take me to the ultimate recipe like you said?!

"Oh yes, yes, of course, but pray don't you want to further spend a spell reclining and relaxing in the opulence of wine and scarves, my dear Soul?"

Well, hey, let me spell this out: "G-E-T-M-E-O-U-T-O-F-H-E-R-E"! I mean, no offense, but I've got an ultimate recipe to discover and after this I just want to go home and have a bag of chips and a beer and listen to some rock and roll!

"Oh dear, yes, very well then my dear relaxed Soul, we shall you away anon!"

Uh-huh.

And with (you guessed it) a great pompous fanfare, their harp-strewn, gorging 'pon plums and dumplings, wine and honey procession proceeded achingly slowly down the carpeted highway. How do they keep that thing clean? Everyone was on a pile of silk and gold pillows on top of an ornate litter– who's even carrying these things down there? Hmmm, maybe we're floating–must be the harp music, yeah that works!

The fine golden glow began to morph into what was obviously regular sunlight. "Farewell fair Soul-Chef" they waved sadly, wiping tears precisely with their embroidered scarves. "We can go no further, simply cross the plateau and climb the mountain path and voila– a very old Soul has what you seek, farewell, oh do return for some scrumptious morsels and divine waters some time…" as they applauded incessantly. Buh-bye! I gave 'em a hearty wave and turned, whistling on the way as I trekked across the fine rock, happy to be alive, on my way, and not walking on pillows!

After a spell (now I'm talking like them!) the music faded into the wind. Ooh, a little cold, getting dark, I can't really see up ahead. Maybe I'll just take a rest, build a fire and cook a little something from these things they gave me– ooh truffles, they didn't bust these out before! Ah yes, this smell is divine, I think my cooking has taken a cosmic leap due to this blasted adventure! Can't wait to get the uh-uh-ultimate re-ci-i-i-i-pee! *Doot doot…doot… doot?* Uh oh, what is that whirring sound? It's getting louder! Flashing lights? What the– it can't be? A craft! It's gonna land– of course! Damn and I haven't even eaten my dinner yet! Of course, of course this is happening, how could it not go down like this? Bottom of the sea, Greek weirdos in the middle of the earth and now freaking Aliens! I won't even bother running this time, and oh gee I wonder what they want.

"THUNK!"

Oh, "good". They've landed! Look just like the pictures too, only uglier– grey one, green one, blue one. All skinny with big heads. What, no lizard man? Hey, watch it!

"Gleeb sppooob!"

Well, I'm glad you're so delighted but that's my dinner! Hey, hands offa that! No, I'm hungry! No don't eat it! Too late!!! "Argaaaah Gedaaaaahhh!", they jumped up and down with glee, devouring every last morsel, practically high-fiving each other as they looked at me inquisitively… "Arp sclav!"

No, no, no,no I'm not getting in that thing!

"Skeeb skeeb!" they pushed me insistently toward the craft as the engine began to rev up. Got plans do we? Well so do I… then again, what's another sidebar in this crazy quest…

The Flavored Waters

They drank I thought excessively of fresh water steeped with 1, 2 or 3 of these ingredients in any combination they saw fit: orange, grapefruit, lemon, lime, cucumber, anise, vanilla, coconut, pineapple, pomegranate, cinnamon, rosemary, lavender, rose petals, kiwi, mango, peach, sage, melon, mint, basil, tangerine, ginger, lychee, green and red bell peppers, thyme, violet, pear, plum, raspberry, apricots, carrot, cilantro, strawberry, lemongrass, even sweet onion and horseradish!

They were all quite refreshing. At night they stewed these things in pots of tea or simply added spears to their cups. They seeded and peeled as they saw fit, for some have too bitter a rind or seeds. Of pomegranates, they used the seeds and juice only. Delicious.

Try this at home.

PENNE WITH SQUASH AND WINE MARINARA SAUCE

3 cups chopped squash
1 diced onion
3 or 4 minced garlic cloves
2 cups crushed tomatoes
¼ cup tomato paste
¼ cup each chopped oregano, rosemary
Salt and pepper
1 cup red wine
Several tablespoon soy sauce
1 teaspoon each chili powder, paprika,
cumin and coriander
2 chopped bell peppers
¼ cup olive oil
A few tablespoon red wine vinegar
A little broth as needed
Penne

Roast the squash at 375° for half an hour
or so, coated in a little olive oil, salt and
pepper with a bit of water. Turn once.
Remove from oven and set aside for the
moment.

Begin cooking onion and garlic in some
olive oil for two minutes with a little salt
and pepper. Add squash, crushed tomatoes,
half of the herbs and half of the spices
with half of the wine and some soy sauce
and cook for 5 minutes. Add the peppers,
tomato paste, rest of the spices, salt and
pepper, the rest of the soy sauce, vinegar
and the rest of the herbs plus a little broth,
and mash the squash up with a whisk or
masher. Cook, simmering for 15 minutes
adding a little more wine every once in a
while. Season again to taste and cook 5
minutes more. Cook and drain the penne
and toss it with some salt, pepper and
margarine or olive oil and serve with this
marinara on top.

BASIL ZUCCHINI FINGERS

Several firm zucchini, cut into thick sticks
½ cup flour, ½ cup rice flour
½ teaspoon baking powder
2 tablespoon lemon juice
3 or 4 cloves minced garlic, 1 teaspoon
garlic powder
1 cup chopped basil
1½ teaspoon chili powder
Salt and pepper to taste
Olive oil

Coat the zucchini with lemon juice and
olive oil, sprinkle with salt and pepper.
Dredge thru a mixture of the flours, baking
powder, chili powder and garlic powder
and some salt and pepper. Place in a
greased baking dish in a single layer on
top of half of the basil, and top with the
minced garlic, sprinkle with a little olive oil.
Broil for about 10 minutes.

Decorate the plate with extra basil. I like
to serve it with a vegan mayonnaise with
extra lemon juice and some curry powder
in it.

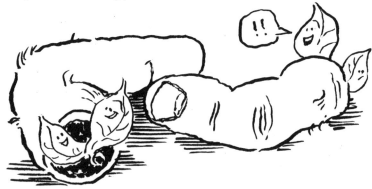

Asian Pear and Plum Wedges Wrapped in Veggie Ham and Basil Leaves, with Pom and Sesame Sauce

Asian pears
Red plums
Balsamic vinegar
Salt and pepper
Veggie "ham"
Basil leaves
Toasted sesame seeds

Take wedges of asian pears and firm red plums, coat them in a little balsamic vinegar, sprinkle with salt and pepper. Wrap each wedge in a basil leaf and a veggie "ham" slice.

Don't like fake meat? Try roasted eggplant, seasoned tofu or tempeh). Secure with a toothpick and sprinkle with toasted sesame seeds. Chill.

How about this for a sauce?

2 tablespoon pomegranate juice, ½ teaspoon sesame seeds, 1 tablespoon soy sauce, 2 teaspoon Chinese black vinegar, 1 teaspoon lemon juice, 1 teaspoon sesame oil, and a little chili sauce if desired.

Mushroom Caps Stuffed with Pesto

1 or 2 dozen large crimini for stuffing
½ cup chopped toasted pine nuts
½ cup minced basil
¼ cup minced flat parsley
4 minced garlic cloves
½ cup minced onion
2 to 3 tablespoon lemon juice
Salt and pepper, a little bit of chili flakes
2 tablespoon minced sage
½ cup vegan cream cheese
1 tablespoon flour
¼ cup olive oil

Mix all but the mushrooms together (you can blend it in a food processor or have it be a little rustic mince going on as is), save a little olive oil and some salt and pepper. Take the stems out of the mushrooms, then stuff them with the mixture. Place them in a casserole, sprinkle with a little salt, pepper and olive oil and put a tablespoon of water in the pan. Bake at 375° for 20 minutes (or just broil them for 10 minutes, even better!). Ta-da!

CUCUMBER, ROASTED PEPPERS, GRAPES AND OLIVES WITH HERBED LEMON DRESSING IN ENDIVE CUPS

2 cups halved seedless grapes
2 sliced cucumbers, stripe them if you like
2 cups roasted bell, sweet and hot peppers, cut into strips
½ cup chopped pitted olives
¼ cup minced red onion
Salt and pepper
Juice of 2 or 3 lemons
½ cup minced herbs (dill, parsley, tarragon are nice)
Several tablespoon olive oil
½ teaspoon each fennel seed, chili powder, paprika
A pinch of crushed saffron
A little sugar
A dash of sumac powder
A little white balsamic or red wine vinegar and a bit of tahini sauce or dressing to taste
1 tablespoon pomegranate syrup/ concentrate
1 or 2 tablespoon capers– always good
Endive leaves (roundly fellowes for serving use as cups)

Mix all but the endive together and chill.

Serve in endive cups.

Chilled Asparagus in Orange Vinaigrette

2 lbs. asparagus spears
2 tablespoon shaved onion
1 seeded, shredded orange
¼ cup orange juice
1 or 2 teaspoon grated orange peel
Lemon juice and red wine vinegar to taste
Salt and pepper
¼ cup chopped chervil
A little sugar or ginger syrup
2 to 3 tablespoon olive oil
½ teaspoon crushed mustard seed
Cointreau
Option: add toasted pine nuts or sunflower
seeds to the serving

Blanch the asparagus spears, drain with
some ice cubes to cool quickly. Mix the
rest (except liqueur) to make a sauce
and then toss with the asparagus and
chill. Serve chilled with a little Cointreau
sprinkled on top.

RED WINE SORBET *with* CHOCOLATE CROSTINI, BERRIES IN LIQUEUR AND CHOCOLATE-BALSAMIC REDUCTION

1 cup red wine
2 cups vanilla soy creamer
½ teaspoon greated nutmeg
1 cup sugar
Vanilla
2 or 3 tablespoon lemon juice
A few tablespoon blackberry juice
Pinch or two salt

Melt sugar in wine over low/med heat with nutmeg and then allow to cool. Blend with everything in batches and freeze, stirring every now and then to prevent hard freezing. This will take some time to freeze properly, because of the wine. It need only be modestly firm.

Baguette
Chocolate
Sugar
A little almond milk
Oil
Toast baguette slices brushed with a little oil and sugar. Dip them in the chocolate melted with a splash of almond milk and cool. Serve with the rest.

Berries
Crème de cassis
Cinnamon sugar

Here mix all of your favorite berries with liqueur and cinnamon sugar and serve with the rest.

1 cup balsamic vinegar
A little sugar
Some chocolate (bittersweet)

Heat 1 cup balsamic vinegar with a little additional sugar to it. Simmer for about 20 minutes or until you note that it has reduced to a more syrupy state. Remove from heat and shave in ¼ cup of chocolate. Stir until it has melted. Cool to room temperature, whisking to make sure it doesn't separate too severely and serve with the rest.

A little orange or lemon peel grated about the whole business is a delight.

FRIED VEGGIE CAKES IN SAMBUCA SAUCE WITH FIG RELISH

½ cup chopped onion
2 minced garlic cloves
2 teaspoon minced ginger
1 tablespoon olive oil
½ cup sambuca
¼ cup orange juice
A little sugar
Salt and pepper to taste
½ teaspoon fennel seed
A little cumin seed
A pinch of cloves and allspice
Flour or cornstarch to thicken (use only a little at a time)

This is the sauce. Cook the onions, ginger and garlic in oil with the seeds until lightly browned, then add the sugar, orange juice and sambuca and cook for several minutes more. It can be thickened with a small amount of cornstarch or flour.

Serve with these cakes:

1 cup chopped roasted eggplant
½ cup sliced fennel
1 minced carrot
¼ cup roasted sunflower seeds
1 minced red bell pepper
1 tablespoon oil
½ cup chopped parsley
¼ cup chopped herbs
¼ cup chopped mushrooms
½ cup chopped red onion

1 cup flour (more to make the cakes firm if needed)
1 teaspoon baking powder
1 teaspoon each coriander, cumin and turmeric
½ cup orange juice
A few tablespoon Sambuca
Salt and pepper to taste

Mix together, adding more liquid or flour if needed to make a drop batter (pretty thick). Season it more if you want to. Fry in some oil (doesn't have to be that deep), as little cakes, turning once, brown on both sides.

For the relish:

1 cup chopped figs
½ cup chopped oranges (seeded, peeled)
1 teaspoon grated orange peel
1 teaspoon minced ginger
¼ cup chopped toasted pecans
¼ cup chopped red onion
¼ cup chopped basil
½ cup chopped parsley
2 tablespoon minced oregano
1 chopped red bell pepper
2 tablespoon (or more) balsamic vinegar
Salt and pepper, tamari to taste
2 tablespoon walnut oil
1½ teaspoon Persian spice mix (panch phoran)
A little rose water or orange blossom water
Juice of 1 lemon
Mix together and serve with cakes.

They weren't taking no for an answer.

"Zglark xoob!"

Okay, okay here I go. Stop pointing those things at me. I'm not sure what they do but I know I don't like it!

"Zggagg dormf!"

Guess I'm going into space– got any Dramamine? I was marched onto the shuttle as they chattered excitedly.

They sat me down.

No seat belt?

"Whoopf!"

(Oof! Sorry I asked, there it is.)

And we blasted off in a whirring kaleidoscope of streaming light and color– I swear is that? Is that a carrot? Into a great cloud of half eaten and discarded earth vegetables and fruits, a scattered puddle of cream floating about unappetizingly. Culinary flotsam and jetsam mixed in with the satellites– uh oh looks like somebody has been doing some failed experiments!

From out of this mess we emerged, getting nearer then into… into a strange flying teacup and saucer, bleep-bloop flashing with gumdrop lights and licorice neon. Once inside, I hopped out on to the glittery tarmac and sure enough, here came the pompous sort of procession I had grown accustomed to by now– the same on any planet, it's got to be the boss! They floated out in a great drove, their wispy limbs bearing strange new galactic gastronomical delights (and horrors), and I gratefully devoured each new experience as their leader (a very bulbous-headed green and gold fellow, must be the large brain) garbled on and on about their great plan and our future utopian world which we would share with them when the time was right and how I was special because the food seemed close to theirs and they needed me to help hybrid their bizarre dishes with our cuisine in order for them to communicate properly in the universal language (food, of course!) with our leaders and would I assist and blah blah blah!

"Skkeepb blarf glop gleev"

He seemed a little cross (although the intrinsically harsh language made it awful hard to tell) that they kept faiing to be able to figure out how to use the earth ingredients properly. Thus, in a fit, he would order the disastrous results of their cooking tragedies jettisoned every time! Good grief- what's that crazy burning smell? Tofu?

"Ka-BOOOM!"

"Yarg blarg, aieeee!", squealing aliens on fire were running all about and a billowing cloud of oil smoke filled the room.

"Kack-ack! Gugh uch!"

They reeled and fled as though from an oncoming invasion.

"See what I mean?!?! You have to help us!", the chief emoted, finally using telepathy

I had a mouthful of something that seemed like comet tails. Was this still moving? Ugh! Yeah, sure thing buddy, I always aim to please. Just don't put your ray gun to my head and it'll be smooth cruising in the cosmic kitchen!

They seemed to be afraid of offending our bosses with some of the absolutely hideous-looking things they were carting in from all over the galaxy– even the vegetables had tentacles that kept grabbing me, let alone their own terrible odes to earth ingredients… (One bum note after another!). Not half bad though, some of the alien stuff. Too bad I had a quest to finish, otherwise I would have liked to take a look at those interplanetary markets. They had utensils and cooking methods that I probably will never understand. Laser-cooked is a lot faster than even induction. Now there's a use we can all agree on! They could also cook with music, blaring or tooting through some weird pan flute to merge the sounds with the ingredients until they intertwined

with each other, creating some new combination. Hey– no fair!

For some reason everything they were eating it seemed (practically) tasted of bananas. They kinda like bananas.

They were keeping an eye on us and our food through a vast but poorly translated surveillance system, mimicking our dishes using their ingredients.

I saw them make a grilled cheese with the cheese on the outside– what a mess! Well, I did what I could for them and took a lot to heart about their own style as well.

After all of this back and forth, I soon appreciated that they seemed to be making sure we humans didn't "burn down the whole kitchen". I almost started to like the place. But soon we reached the limit of our transaction, and my reward was forthcoming. With a handy dandy shuttle ship and a "Ark Jarg gok Spleeb!", they took me to my final destination and dropped me off. After all of their surveillance, they seemed to think they had a line on the recipe's location.

As I strode out of the craft, waving over my shoulder, I was suddenly chilled by a blast of cold air– what the…?!?! Where's all the oxygen too, for that matter– the air's a little thin for the earth isn't it?! Where did you bozos bring me, who the hell is out here, cooking anything? Ice, cold, nothing growing– a mountaintop, Himalayalayaz??!

"Yes, yes, high mountains", they warbled in
their best English, "Yes, yes, Yeti, snowman"

Frosty? Wait, Yeti? Uh, oh, not the ... the...
Abominable Snowman! I'm getting back on
the ship, no, wait!

"Yes, yes, Yeti!"

No, no Yeti!

"Yes yes, bye bye, Snow Chef, Yes yes Yeti
soon soon...Farewell..."

Too late, they sped off, up and darted out
of site.

No sooner than they departed, a hulking
shadow lurched out from behind a huge
icy rock and loomed over me, before I
could even react...

Zagort Skibort
(no equivalent English translation!)

Mix 1 cup shredded cucumber, ¼ cup grated carrot, 1 tablespoon grated ginger, 2 tablespoon lemon or lime juice, 2 cups coconut milk mixed with a banana, ½ teaspoon cardamom, a little salt, a little sugar and a little cinnamon, ½ teaspoon nigella seed (kalonji)

Drink up with ice– ewww… the stringy cucumber is scary!

SPICY BANANA POCKETS (SKLORT STEEB)

Eggroll/wonton wrappers
1 cup mashed bananas
¼ cup grated coconut
¼ cup minced onion
2 minced garlic cloves
1 tablespoon grated ginger
1 tablespoon chili garlic sauce
Soy sauce and rice vinegar to taste
A little mint, basil and cilantro
½ teaspoon minced lemongrass
1 or 2 jalepenos or fresnos, sliced into rings
A little sugar
1 teaspoon garam masala
1 tablespoon peanut oil
A few tablespoon of some shredded vegetable– carrot or daikon
Oil for frying

Mix all but the wrappers and frying oil together. There was something stringy in there, this will work– you could also try shredded jicama, mung bean sprouts or bamboo. Place a dollop of this stuff on a wrapper, roll it up nice and tight and fry them in oil (doesn't have to be super deep if you turn them!) until browned all about. Serve with hoisin or black bean-garlic sauce and some chili sauce.

This had a strange taste, difficult to mimic but I believe this will work as an approximation– add some fennel seeds to really get the drift!

SCALLOPED PINEAPPLE AND TOMATO SLICES (ADGVAK-VADDA VAK)

1 pineapple, peeled, cored and cut into slices and drained
2 tomatoes, ripe but very firm, cut into thin slices and drained
1 sliced red onion
$1/3$ cup chopped cilantro
1 teaspoon chili powder
1 cup seasoned breadcrumbs
Up to ½ cup margarine/oil
Salt and pepper to taste
½ cup chopped parsley
Up to ½ cup flour
½ cup cashew milk
2 teaspoon curry powder
2 tablespoon lemon juice
2 or 3 thinly sliced garlic cloves

In a greased casserole, layer pineapple and tomato slices with the onions, garlic cloves, cilantro and parsley, sprinkling each layer with a little lemon juice, flour, salt and pepper, chili powder and curry powder and dotting with a bit of margarine or oil. Mix together cashew milk with 2 tablespoon of flour, some salt and pepper and a little curry powder and pour over the whole mixture. Dot with a little margarine again, cover in breadcrumbs, sprinkle that with a little curry powder and bake at 375° for about 40 minutes or until the top is browned.

A bit gelatinous here and there but still good. Can be served hot or cold. They ate something similar for breakfast which was on a cosmic clock (no sunrise up there!)

Spicy Cold Tomato-Pepper Soup with Chopped Toasted Peanuts and Cucumber Jelly (Grakgebak Hak Akgebak)

4 cups broth with 1 tablespoon ginger grated into it
½ cup pineapple juice
1 cup ground tomatoes
2 chopped, seeded, drained tomatoes
2 cups roasted red peppers, sliced
2 chili peppers, minced
½ cup grated carrots
1 minced onion
½ cup mixed herbs: chervil, oregano, cilantro, basil, dill
salt and pepper to taste
1½ teaspoon chili powder
1 teaspoon each cumin, coriander, turmeric and fennel
Hot sauce, chili sauce to taste

Mix all of this together and allow to sit for a few hours. You can have as is with the garnishes or then simmer it for 30 minutes and chill or serve hot, any of those three ways, and you know we adventurers love three ways!

Garnish with even more fresh veggies and chopped cucumber or pineapple if you have them and chopped cilantro and roasted salted peanuts.

And this jelly:

Blend ¼ cup coconut, ¼ cup oil, ¼ cup sugar, ½ cup coconut milk, 1 teaspoon cornstarch and a little broth.

Heat over medium, stirring, until thickened a bit.

Now add 1 cup of peeled, seeded, shredded or grated cucumber. Add salt and a little cloves or nutmeg, and a few pinches of allspice with a bit of whole toasted cumin or celery seed to taste. Chill and serve with soup.

I ate the most normal thing of the journey, a strange dark grain-like substance that they paired with crunchy chunks. It's reminiscent of water chestnut but sharper. They claimed it was a hard space jelly and anti-matter. But what the hell do they know?

This is better...

BLACK RICE WITH CUBED DAIKON (GAR BAK DARF WOOG)

1½ cup black rice
Broth
1 chopped onion
1 cup diced daikon or water chestnut
1 or 2 minced garlic cloves
1 or 2 tablespoon sesame oil
¼ cup chopped toasted pecans
¼ cup chopped parsley
Salt and pepper
Additions: sautéed mushrooms with sesame seeds, chopped basil or cilantro or other herb, diced carrots. Add at the end.

Cook black rice according to instructions in broth, with sesame oil, garlic, and onion added to it, plus some salt and pepper. When cooked (and drained if necessary), add daikon, pecans and parsley and re-season (sprinkle with a little salt or soy sauce) and then allow to sit for a few minutes before serving.

This was like a horror show but tasted great!

HIJIKI, WAKAME, MUSHROOM, FUNGUS AND SQUASH SALAD (ZAMMA ZAK HEFLACK)

Hijiki (½ cup, reconstituted in tea, chopped if you want to)
Wakame (1 cup reconstituted in miso soup, chopped)
1 cup chopped black fungus
¼ cup chopped Chinese moss
2 carrots, cut into thin half moons
2 cups squash, cut into thin half moons and blanched and drained (1 or 2 min. in boiling water)
2 minced scallions
2–3 tablespoon plum vinegar
2 tablespoon sesame oil
2 teaspoon black sesame seeds
1 or 2 tablespoon grated ginger
Soy sauce to taste

Toss it all together and allow flavors to mingle, then toss again and re-season. You may add mizuna or watercress or something to make it more of an earthly salad.

One of them reached out its tentacle beyond the force field encasing the ship, snared a chunk of the nearest system and whapped it back down onto a plate and something like this appeared:

Adajak Schlark Eebsblagk, translates as "Fragrant Galaxy"

Serve with a lightly seasoned black or red rice.

Several lbs. firm, seasoned tofu– cut this into slices and then into stars using a cookie cutter. Save the odd pieces to make a scramble or something another time.

Now, marinate the tofu in:
½ cup soy sauce
2 or 3 tablespoon finely grated ginger
6 pressed cloves of garlic
1 finely minced onion
¼ cup rice vinegar
2 or 3 tablespoon sesame oil
2 or 3 tablespoon peanut or sunflower oil
Ambitious? Separate the tofu into three groups and baste each with a bit of purée of the three sauces below!
Allow these to sit for a little while. Then dredge the pieces in breadcrumbs (fine seasoned panko is great) and fry in fairly shallow oil, turning, until browned on both sides. Serve on plates with your special rice, these three sauces arrayed, and some decorative orange, green, red and black items (preferably edilble!).

All three of these sauces, make in any of these ways:

Mix together or blend together and either heat with a bit of broth or juice (add just a little at first, to control the consistency when the fruit cooks down), stirring, until cooked to your liking– make sure to adjust seasonings to taste. Or you can cook as is more like relish/salsa sauces with out adding more liquid. Or you can blend or keep as is and chill these items and serve with the tofu.

Red
2 or 3 minced hot chilies
½ cup passion fruit pulp or jam (no seeds)
1 cup chopped strawberries
¼ cup lime juice
2 teaspoon red curry powder
1 teaspoon chili powder
½ teaspoon cumin
¼ cup minced red onion
Salt and pepper to taste

Green
1 cup chopped kiwi fruit
1 teaspoon, ground coriander
1 or 2 tablespoon green curry paste
1 diced green pepper
$^1/_3$ cup lime juice
A little sweetener if needed
Salt and pepper to taste (I favor green peppercorns for this)
2 minced garlic cloves
Chopped cilantro and basil

Orange
1 cup chopped mango
¼ cup pineapple juice
¼ cup grated carrot
½ teaspoon cloves
1 teaspoon turmeric
2 tablespoon sugar or rice syrup
1 chopped habenero

½ cup minced onion
Salt to taste
Add a little orange bell pepper if you like

Again with the bananas, but doesn't
everything weird taste like bananas? This
was like spaghetti but you earth people
should have it for dessert, it's quite simple.

BANANA NOODLES ON COCONUT CREAM WITH CHOPPED TROPICAL FRUIT AND PAPAYA "ICE CREAM" GUNCHA GLRAGROK

1 bunch firm, ripe bananas
Lime juice, sugar, salt
Cut these into long, noodle-like strips and coat with sugar, lime juice and a pinch of salt.

1 cup thick coconut cream
A few tablespoon sugar
½ teaspoon vanilla
A few pinches of cardamom
Mix this and chill.

Now mix ½ cup or so each chopped mango, papaya, strawberries sprinkle with sugar, lime juice, a few pinches of cardamom and cinnamon, chill.

Make an ice cream by blending:
1 cup papaya,
2 tablespoon rum,
¼ cup sugar
½ cup chopped mango
¼ cup orange juice
Innards of 1 vanilla bean
½ cup coconut milk
Pinch of salt
A little lime juice if you like

Freeze this, mixing it again every once in a while, until it is ready (It's up to you when).

To serve, place some coconut cream mixture in a bowl. Place some banana noodles on this, with fruit compote on top, papaya "ice cream" on the side, and garnish with some mint leaves

His big icy, heavy paw came crashing down, I skittered across the ice ledge, practically falling into a huge chasm.

Hey– isn't that the Crusty Cavern down there? Well, I don't need to go back so soon! I pushed back and jumped up to my feet, hunkered down and pulled out my chef's knife. I'll give you a taste you big brute, give me the recipe!

"Mrarr, NEVER!"

He lunged. I dodged. Oh, I'm gonna get it if I have to carve it out of the hide on your back. He tried to clobber me with a huge ice club! I pushed his massive arm up and to the left and the club smashed into the side of the mountain, shattering into a thousalnd pieces. Out tumbled a small bottle– *clink Clank CLUNK*. I scrambled to grab it, he lunged forward– I rolled, got it, rolled again to avoid the next crushing blow. The recipe at last! I popped it open…

"Noooo!" he screamed.

Oops, it's Kahlua.

"For my Mexican coffee, you bastard! Graaaa!"

"Give me the recipe, the ultimate recipe!"

"You'll never get it because I will only tell you if you can defeat me!", shouted the big lummox. He rushed toward me again, knocking me off my feet. Worth the old

college try… I've come so far, even though weakened, exhausted and out of breath, I can't give up now.

He leapt up and prepared to strike.

"I shall remain the greatest chef in the ice, you have made your final dish!", he growled menacingly. (That recipe must be something else!).

I grabbed his arm as it came down, pulling him in suddenly and plunging in my knife with the other hand, pulled my leg up to my chin and kicked him full in the chest. Scooted my body down and rolled over, pushing him ahead of me and, yes success, and…

off the ledge!

Oops, he was supposed to come down hard but not that hard! Damn, now I'll never know, you big oaf!!! There you go, taking your ultimate recipe with you, all of this for… for nothing…

I was about on the edge of tears but then, no, wait… Jeez that IS a long way down… Wait… What is he saying? He's saying something…

As he fell into the chasm, his bellowing abominable voice yowled harshly and then began trailing off:

"No, you DUMMY, the utimate recipe is whatever your favorite thing to eat Is! Just make it veeegaaan… What's that smell? tahini? *IIIIIEEEEEEEEEE!!!*…"

How un-freaking-ceremonious– are you kidding me? No big hoopla, just that simple. It's what I like and it's different for everyone. Gosh, what do I even enjoy eating the most? Pizza? Cake and ice cream? Deep fried shish kebabs? Eggplant parm? Vietnamese crepe? Crepe, Bahn Xao... but it's so eggy... but why wouldn't it work, I certainly do like it!

You know, I never tried to make that one before vegan but hey what the hell...

Shit, that was easy!

After a long tawdry journey home, I made my own "welcome home" feast for the whole gang– just like how I always bake my own birthday cakes. No big deal! They all loved it, and were so excited by my tales of adventure that they never did ask, "What was the Ultimate Recipe after all?".

Really, it just never came up.

All they had to say about this dish was, "Good stuff, JP, old chum! I could eat this everyday!" (Hmmm... is that the point?).

And with that our tale comes to its upbeat close.

Oops, no, wait... I almost forgot...

TOFU CREPE *with* VEGGIE "PORK", FIXINS AND SAUCES

Bahn Xao? Bahn Xao!

For the crepe, blend:
½ cup tofu
1 cup mushroom broth
2 tablespoon melted margarine
1 teaspoon sesame oil
2 crushed garlic cloves
1 teaspoon lemon juice
...until smooth. Now mix in:

1 cup flour
$1/3$ cup rice flour
2 teaspoon yellow curry powder
1 teaspoon salt
2 teaspoon sugar
1 teaspoon baking powder

Form a pancake-like batter. Spread around ½ cup of batter in a medium-hot well-oiled griddle (a little standing grease in there!) to about 8" diameter. Cook until the bubbles appear and you can tell from the edge that it is crispy under there, then flip it and cook the other side.

Serve with these sauces:
• Hoisin or plum sauce
• Chili-garlic Sauce (Sambal) or Cock Sauce
• if you like, this is your "fish sauce":
Mix ½ cup seasoned rice vinegar, 2 teaspoon ground toasted sesame seeds (finely-ground), 2 teaspoon chili sauce and salt to taste, add a little ground or flake seaweed

Accompany with:
Basil leaves
Cilantro
Thinly-sliced red onion
Chopped scallion
Cucumber and daikon cut into strips
Chopped 5-spice tofu
Mung bean sprouts
Roasted peanuts
Julienned carrots

And this:
Make a sauce of your favorite barbecue sauce, soy sauce, 1 tablespoon beet powder, black pepper, hoisin sauce, ketchup and some five-spice. Mix til you are in love with the taste. Coat thoroughly logs/strips (however long and about 2½ to 3 inches thick) of veggie "ham" or "pork"– these come in log form, get those and cut them to size.

Bake in a greased pan with a small amount of water at 375° for about 40 minutes, turning and basting every now and then.

When it's done, cut very thin slices. There is your "barbecue pork" which you can shred or use in slices, serve with the crepe.

To eat this you need some flexible lettuce leaves.

Fill your crepe with the accompaniments and fold in half. Cut pieces off and eat them wrapped in lettuce, dipping in the sauces whenever you please.

Ta-da, the ultimate! Or at least I like it...

Find your own ultimate recipes and share them with me!

NOW the tale comes to a close...

And they all lived happily ever after, except too stuffed to move!

The end?

NOTES

NOTES

NOTES